"The moving story ⌐⌐ ⌐ finds her God-given gift, while coming to terms with loss and change."
~BILL MEYERS,
Author of *Eli* and *The Jesus Experience*

"Young readers will relate to the story of a girl trying to find her place in her family and in the world, and the strong voice and gentle sense of humor will keep them reading. Not to mention a wayward cat and a mystery or two. A fun read with real emotions and good values."
~JEANNIE ST. JOHN TAYLOR,
Radio Host and Author/Illustrator of thirty-plus books

"Delightful characters, realistic situations, and beautifully expressed emotions make *Picture Imperfect* the perfect read."
~ANGELA RUTH STRONG,
Author of The Fun4Hire Series

Picture
Imperfect

Susan Thogerson Maas

To Darlene and
David,
May God bless you
and your family!
Susan Thogerson Maas

Ashberry Lane

© 2015 by Susan Thogerson Maas
Ashberry Lane
P.O. Box 665, Gaston, OR 97119
www.ashberrylane.com
Printed in the United States of America

ISBN 978-1-941720-10-3

Library of Congress Control Number: 2015932917

Cover design by Miller Media Solutions
Photos from www.dollarphotoclub.com

FICTION / Middle Grade

Dedicated to my loving
and supportive husband,
Gary Thogerson

1

The rental truck rumbled into my driveway.

So soon? I grabbed my camera—the one Gram gave me for my 12th birthday—and ran to the kitchen. I had to get a picture of Aunt Melissa stepping into our house. I would call it *The Invasion*.

But Mom would not approve. "Lissa" was her baby sister, after all. Though that baby sister was almost thirty years old.

I'd go with *The Change*.

Mom walked in, followed by Lissa, whose long, golden hair was pulled back in a ponytail. She wore a flowery shirt, tight jeans, and, of all things, high heels.

I pressed the shutter button.

The flash went off and Lissa jumped, tottering for a moment on those narrow heels before regaining her balance. "What was that?" she cried. Then she saw me. "Oh, it's you. I should have known. Hi, Miss Jada Jane." She pulled me to her and smothered me in a hug. "Or should I say 'roomie?'"

I cringed. Calling me by my full name was bad enough but "roomie" was just plain scary. Faking a smile, I snapped another picture. Maybe I *would* call it *The Invasion*.

Mom tromped down the hall, yelling, "Brett! Come on out. We need your help."

My brother emerged from his room in shorts, a

rumpled T-shirt, and flip-flops. His dark, curly hair stuck out on the left side and was plastered down on the right, making it easy to tell which side he'd slept on. He rubbed his eyes and grinned.

I snapped his picture.

Brett stuck his tongue out at me. He didn't really mind his picture being taken, though. After all, that's something a sports star would have to get used to, and he intended to become one.

"You didn't just wake up, did you?" Mom asked. "It's one in the afternoon."

Brett's grin got bigger. "Didn't you read that study about teenagers needing more sleep? I'm a growing boy." He flexed his biceps. "Let me at that furniture. I'm ready."

Laughing, Mom shook her head, then her serious look returned.

Time to work. I stuck my camera in a drawer. Couldn't risk it getting knocked over and broken.

Mom led the way outside to an ugly orange-and-white truck. Dad pulled a cardboard box out of the back and plunked it down next to several others on the cement.

Boxes that would soon invade *my* room.

Dad grunted and wiped the sweat off his forehead.

The early summer sun glared down, but a gentle breeze whispered through my hair and cooled my face. Not bad at all for June. At least it wasn't raining. If it weren't for Aunt Lissa invading our house, it could have been a perfect day.

"Okay," Dad said, "let's get organized. Lissa and Carol, you can take boxes to the bedroom. Brett, you help me with the furniture. We'll put most of it in the basement. JJ, you can take a box, then help Lissa arrange her stuff."

I nodded.

"I want the bed, chair, desk, and dresser in the room," Lissa said.

Dad stared at her.

"Please."

"There's not much space in my room." My stomach twisted. "I don't think they'll fit." Why did I have to share my room? It wasn't fair. Of course, I knew the answer.

She couldn't very well room with Brett, and we didn't have an extra bedroom. Still …

"They'll fit." Lissa stuck her hands on her hips. "I'm going to make the bed into a bunk bed and put the desk and dresser under it. It will be almost like college again."

Dad looked at me, eyebrows raised.

I shrugged. Nobody asked my permission before saying she could move in, so why ask now? Besides, Dad wasn't likely to do anything. It wasn't his room, so what did he care? Mom had better be right about Lissa only staying for a little while.

Dad handed a box to Lissa, then Mom, and then me.

Lissa headed into the house but stopped just inside and propped the door open.

"No," I called. "You can't leave the door open. Tasha will get out."

"Tasha? Who in the world is Tasha?" Lissa gave me a snarky look.

A nasty answer started to bubble up inside me, but I

swallowed it back down. I hated this already. "Tasha is my cat. We can't let her get out."

"Why not? Cats should be able to go where they want, shouldn't they?"

"Tasha is an indoor cat." The box I carried was gaining weight by the moment. What did she have in it, a rock collection? I tried to get a better grip. "Come on. Let's get going."

"Move it." Mom gave Lissa a shove with her box.

Lissa moved on, letting the screen door slam behind her.

"You can't close only the screen door, Lissa," I hollered after her. "Tasha can open screen doors."

Would she remember that important fact when there was nobody else to close the door for her?

I didn't hear an answer, so I closed it and clomped along after Mom. Panting, I set the box down in what had once been *my* room.

Dad and Brett carried in the bed, leaving the desk and chair in the hall. Dad put the bunk bed frame together, while Lissa directed him. She didn't need to worry; I'm sure Dad was better at that than she would ever be. But she still kept careful watch. When that was done, they brought in the desk, chair, and a small dresser.

With furniture and boxes filling up the room, it didn't feel like mine anymore. Lissa's bed hid most of my Ansel Adams poster, his famous black-and-white photograph of Yosemite Park with a big full moon shining over it. I could get lost in that picture, imagining myself wandering through such a beautiful place, my camera shutter clicking away. What would it be like to be able to take such wonderful photographs?

My own photos didn't come close, but I still liked them. I had two of them on the wall. Thank goodness I had moved them to my side of the room, so I could still see Tasha staring at me in one and a peaceful view of the ocean in the other.

And, by the door, hung the picture my great-grandma had painted of a stream flowing through fern-filled woods. Gram had been a painter for over fifty years, and she still painted some in the retirement home. Her paintings felt the way I wanted my photographs to feel, like someone could walk into them and be at peace. She said painting made her feel close to God.

That didn't make sense to me. How could I be close to some spirit up in the sky somewhere?

But Gram looked so happy when she said it that it made me ache inside.

My parents stood outside the bedroom door, watching as Lissa rearranged boxes and tried to unpack her clothes.

Brett strolled in wearing sweatpants and carrying the long bag with all his baseball gear inside. "Gotta leave for practice. Can I borrow the car?"

Dad dug into his pocket and tossed him the keys. "Bring it back in one piece."

Brett shrugged. "I'll do my best," he said with a wink.

"We need to turn in the rental truck." Mom pulled at the corner of Lissa's blouse. "Come on, sis. You're the one paying for it."

Lissa grabbed her purse and followed Mom out the door.

5

Dad slouched in the doorway for another minute or two. He looked sweaty and tired. Being a factory supervisor didn't give him much exercise, I guess, but he'd gotten his full share today. He looked at me, then at Lissa's pile of stuff. "Just what we needed. Another body to take up what little space we have," he muttered. "I hope she can cook."

"She won't be here for long, right? That's what Mom said." Frowning, I twisted a strand of my shoulder-length hair around one finger.

"Only until she gets a job. She promises that won't take long." He stretched and pressed a fist into his lower back. "Hope she's right." He turned and headed down the hall toward the family room. Soon, baseball game sounds blared from the TV. Dad was back in his own world.

If only he cared a little more about mine.

Tasha stared at me from the photo, those big dark eyes watching me, her black-and-white fur so sleek-looking. In my picture she was resting on top of a pile of clean laundry. She should have looked guilty, but she looked like a queen instead. That's why I liked it.

I hadn't seen Tasha since Lissa arrived. She had probably found a quiet place to hide. She wasn't the friendliest cat that ever lived. In fact, Brett called her a black ball of claws.

But she loved me, and I loved her. That was good enough.

I wandered through the house, checking all of Tasha's favorite places—behind the couch, under the beds, in the laundry basket … I stopped for a moment in the living room and looked at the family portrait on the wall. Gram sat in a big chair in the middle, and Dad, Mom, Brett, and I were gathered all around her. I was reaching down to hold her hand. That picture said a lot about our family.

Now Aunt Lissa was shoving her way in. What changes would that bring?

I sighed and moved on. "Tasha!" I called. "Here, kitty, kitty!"

No sign of her.

When I reached the kitchen, I looked under the kitchen table, then turned.

Somebody—most likely somebody named Lissa—had left the door open. And the screen door was slightly ajar.

Oh no.

2

I pushed the screen door open, pulling the other door closed behind me, in case Tasha was still inside.

Fat chance of that. She was always trying to escape to the outdoors to munch on green grass, sniff the flowers, and explore new places.

If I saw her slip out, I could usually catch her easily. She would run down the two stairs and stop at the first patch of grass to take a bite. All I had to do was grab her, along with a few blades of grass to keep her happy.

The problem was I didn't know how long she'd been gone. Had Lissa left the door open now, or had it been open for the last twenty minutes as Dad put the bed together? How far could a cat get in twenty minutes, and which direction would she have gone?

I glanced around.

No sign of a cat.

Why did Lissa have to move in, anyway? Why couldn't she stay in California? *She* might have thought it was a wonderful idea to come back to Oregon and move in with her sister while she looked for work, but it seemed like a really crummy idea to me.

I scoured the backyard, inspecting every bush and looking behind everything from the barbecue to the garbage can.

Still no sign of Tasha.

I called her name over and over.

She never had been good about answering to her name. She was one-hundred-percent cat—doing what she wanted when she wanted, and fully expecting me to feed her on time.

"Tasha!" I trotted into the front yard. There weren't many places to hide in the front.

A dog barked down the street.

I headed toward the sound. Would I find my cat up some tree, too terrified to come down?

"Tasha?"

"Hey, JJ, looking for something?"

I wheeled around, and a big smile came over my face and moved on to fill me up.

There were my two best friends—Katelyn, known as Kat, holding a cat known as Tasha.

"Thank you, thank you, thank you!" I ran down the sidewalk to meet them.

My cat's eyes were wide, and her ears laid back. When Kat handed her to me, Tasha tried to burrow into my arms.

I cuddled her and talked gently. "It's okay, sweetie. You're safe now. No cars or big, bad dogs to bother you."

"She didn't get far," Kat said. "I saw her out my window. I didn't know it was her at first, but I came out to check, and sure enough ... She was one scared kitty. She tried to scratch me, but I got ahold of her before she could."

"I'm so glad you saw her." I rubbed my nose against Tasha's soft fur. "Lissa left the door open." I glared down the street. "Just wait until she gets back."

"Your aunt's here now?" Kat twisted her mouth

9

into an exaggerated frown. "Fun and games! Lightning and thunder!"

"Yeah," I said as we walked back to my house. "Lightning and thunder is more likely than fun and games. Things aren't starting off so great."

Kat bent her fingers into claws, fingernails shiny with black nail polish which matched her black hair and her black T-shirt.

Yep, she kinda liked black.

"Think of it." She raised her eyebrows and lowered her voice. "If it gets too bad, you could always do science experiments on her. Dr. Jekyll and Ms. Hyde, maybe. Or you could drop Tasha on her in the middle of the night. That would be a shock."

Laughing, we walked in the back door and I closed it carefully behind me. I got out a can of Tasha's favorite cat food—tuna, of course. She deserved a treat after her little ordeal.

"I'm bored. Wanna go over to the school and swing or something?" Kat jumped up on the counter and kicked her legs back and forth. "Or we could walk up to the store and get an ice cream bar."

"Maybe. But I have to wait until Mom and Lissa get back. I'm afraid she'll leave the door open again." I pulled my camera out of the drawer and crouched down near Tasha, bringing her into focus. When she looked over at me and licked her face, I snapped the picture. *The Queen Enjoying Her Feast.*

She took a few more bites, then stalked haughtily down the hall, probably to take a nap and recover.

While we waited for Mom and Lissa to return, Kat showed me the new song-and-dance routine she was working on. "I'm going to make it on one of those singing shows eventually. I'll win first prize and a big, fat recording contract. I merely need to practice."

The problem was she didn't look at all like anyone who had ever won—being a bit chubby, with acne, and wearing all that black. Her singing voice was nice, but it might not be good enough to make up for the rest.

Of course, I didn't tell her that. A girl needs her dreams.

Besides, we'd been friends since second grade, and I liked her just the way she was. She was beautiful inside, so who cared what some stupid TV guy thought?

Midway through her song, the television in the other room got louder.

I leaned forward until Dad came into view.

He looked at me with eyebrows raised.

Apparently he didn't appreciate Kat's song.

I smiled at him.

He turned the sound up a bit more.

I chuckled quietly so Kat wouldn't hear.

Probably no need to worry. She was in her own world as she danced around the kitchen, roaring out her song.

Mom's car pulled into the driveway.

Arms crossed, I stood there and waited for the guilty party to enter the room.

Mom came in first, saw me, and stopped.

Lissa almost ran into her, then stepped around and looked back and forth from me to Kat.

Mom tilted her head. "What's the problem?"

"Why don't you ask Kat what she found down the street?"

11

Mom turned to Kat. "Okay, what did you find down the street?"

"Tasha." Kat paused as if to build dramatic effect, eyebrows raised. "And she looked really scared."

Mom turned back to me, an alarmed look on her face. "Is Tasha all right?"

"Yes. But she shouldn't have been outside. *Somebody* left the door open." I stared pointedly at Lissa.

"How do you know it was me?" Lissa's voice rose a bit. "It could have been anyone."

I looked at Mom. "Who was the last one out when you left to take the truck back?"

Mom looked at Lissa.

"That's what I thought." I took a deep breath. "Aunt Melissa, I asked you to keep the door shut. If you leave the door open, you need to lock the screen door."

"Who do you think you are, my mother?" Lissa's voice grew even louder. "So I forgot. I just got here. I can't remember everything. It was an accident." She glared right back at me.

"All right, girls." Mom lifted a hand. "Let's take it easy. JJ, I'm sure Lissa didn't mean to do it."

I opened my mouth to object, but Mom raised her other hand.

"And Lissa, remember that you are a guest here and need to be considerate of others—particularly your new roommate." Mom winked at me.

Different expressions rippled across Lissa's face like waves on the beach, until she settled on a forced smile. "Okay, I'm sorry." At least she sounded a little sincere. "I'll be more careful." She looked questioningly at

Mom.

Who looked at me.

"Okay," I finally said. "I'll forgive you this time."

"Great," the invader said, without much enthusiasm. "Well, I need to go unpack." She flounced down the hall.

Mom patted my back. "I know it's hard, JJ, but hang in there. It's only for a little while."

"Are you sure?"

A flash of uncertainty crossed her face, but she quickly pasted the smile back on. "Well, mostly sure. Lissa's a smart lady, and she should find a job soon. I mean, after all, she has a degree from Princeton. Things will work out."

"That's what my mom said before Dad left us," Kat said.

Mom gave her one of those "please don't" looks, but Kat smiled, picked up the newspaper from the counter, and faked interest in it.

Mom shook her head and walked into the family room. She and Dad started talking quietly.

Was it about me? Sometimes I felt like more of a problem than an asset to the family. Dad was a supervisor at the factory, Mom was getting her teaching degree, and Brett was a sports star. Even Lissa had graduated from a top college. I got Bs and Cs in school, didn't play sports, and certainly would never be a teacher. Just an ordinary, nothing-special kid.

"Hey, did you see this?" Kat held up the newspaper.

"What? The story about the crooked politician or the one about cleaning up pollution?"

"No, buried in the metro section. Look." She

13

handed me the paper, pointing to a little article at the bottom of the second page.

"County Fair to Host Photo Contest," the small headline read.

3

I tingled inside like little bubbles were coursing through my body. The contest would be in two weeks. There were several categories, including some for kids, with small cash prizes. Even better, a big camera shop in town had donated the grand prize—a brand-new digital SLR camera. My dream camera! Oh, the pictures I could take if I turned in my point and shoot for a DSLR.

Images of mountains and flowers and crashing waves danced before my eyes.

The SLR, or "single lens reflex," meant that the picture would end up more like what it showed in the viewfinder. However it worked, I could do a lot with it. I could change settings, edit pictures while still in the camera, and get higher-quality photographs than possible with a cheapo camera like mine. I would finally be able to show my family what I could do. "Use my God-given talent," as Gram would say.

"Well, what do you think?" A triumphant grin spread across Kat's face.

I pumped my fist in the air. "Yes! I'm going to win it!"

Kat danced around in excitement. "I know you can do it. You're the best picture taker I know."

"Photographer, if you please." I lifted my chin and strutted around like some kind of hotshot.

Kat punched me in the gut.

"Unnecessary. Totally unnecessary." I grabbed for her. She jumped out of reach, so I chased her around the room. When I caught her, I tickled her until she fell on the floor, laughing. I plopped down beside her.

"Oh, that hurts!" she cried between laughs.

I jumped up and grabbed my camera off the counter. "Come on. Time to go get some pictures."

"Don't you mean photographs?"

I pretended to tickle her, advancing with my fingers wiggling.

"Pictures will do," she said. "Let's go get some *pictures!*"

I stuck my head into the family room, where Dad was still watching baseball and Mom was looking at a magazine. "I'm going out with Kat to take pictures, okay?"

Dad glanced over, then looked back at the game.

Mom smiled. "Sure. Have fun. Don't go too far."

We headed out the back door, careful to shut it behind us.

Okay, what kind of picture would be likely to win a prize? I could enter a picture in every kids' category. That would help my odds of winning. But where to start?

"What should I take pictures of, Kat?" She had studied contests a lot.

"Let's go over to the school. We could swing while we think."

We crossed the street to the school I had attended from kindergarten through fifth grade. Living right across the street had always made me "special"—I

16

could even go home for lunch. Well, at least when Mom wasn't working.

The old school still brought back memories of learning the letter sounds by cutting out pictures from magazines and gluing them onto construction paper, or banging rhythm sticks together to learn syllables. Grade school had been a lot more fun than middle school.

"Stop, Kat." I stared at the red-brick walls and big windows of the school. "One category was 'buildings.' I could take some pics of the school."

Kat frowned. "Schools are boring. You want to find a purple house or something. Or maybe some of those skyscrapers in downtown Portland."

"Well, I can't get downtown today, and I haven't seen any purple houses in the neighborhood. I've got to start someplace."

"Good point. Let's do it."

Now to decide the angle. A picture of the school from the front would be boring. How could I make it different? "Help me think of something creative. Judges always like creative things. Remember that poetry contest you won last year? Everybody else wrote about puppies or the ocean or love, but you wrote about mold and fungi. The judge said it was the most creative poem he had ever seen."

"That was good, wasn't it?" Kat blew on her fingernails, then put her hands on her hips, trying to look important.

It didn't quite work so I laughed.

She raised her hand to her chin and scrunched up her face, as if thinking took a lot of effort. "You've got to make it unique."

"Yeah." I walked around the building, looking for interesting angles.

At least my memory card could hold lots of pictures. I didn't have to find the perfect one right away. I could keep trying until something worked.

I lay on my back and looked up at the school, getting a bug's-eye view. I took pictures from the corners and close-ups of a patch of bricks and a single window.

None of that seemed super creative.

"I need a photo from the roof looking down. That would be different."

"Good idea." Kat nodded. "But how do you get up there?"

"We have a ladder in the garage." I grinned at Kat, and we took off running for my house. "Make sure nobody sees us," I warned as we crept into the garage. "Somehow I have a feeling Mom and Dad would *not* approve."

"Um, probably not."

We found the ladder—a nice, tall, aluminum one— and carried it out of the garage, closing the door behind us. Kat took one end, and I took the other after jamming my camera in my pants' pocket. We walked slowly to the street, keeping a close eye on the house.

No movement there. Good.

We marched across the street and around to the back of the school. Thankfully, no one was playing on the playground, probably because it was getting pretty hot now in the late afternoon. A little sweat trickled down my forehead, and I stopped to wipe it off with the back of my hand.

We set the ladder near a corner of the school, behind some bushes that would pretty much hide it from view.

I adjusted it until it felt steady. "Okay, hold on," I told Kat.

She moved behind the ladder and grabbed onto the sides. "Ready, set, go."

After making sure the camera was still securely in my pocket, I started up the ladder. I wasn't afraid of heights. In fact, I rather liked being up above things, looking down. Maybe someday I would try hang gliding. Probably after I grew up, since Mom would never allow it.

I made it up to roof level and carefully swung one leg over. The shingles felt secure enough—not slippery or anything. Still holding to the ladder with one hand, I swung the second leg over. I crouched down and looked out over the playground. "Nice view, but I think I'll go up to the top."

"Okay. But don't fall off. I don't want to have to explain it to your folks."

"Don't worry. I wouldn't want to break my camera—or myself." I crawled on hands and knees, just to be extra careful, to the peak and sat down, straddling the roof. I pulled out my camera and snapped a couple of pics—first of the playground below, then of the roof itself with the trees showing in the distance.

I turned around to face the other way and scooted myself bit by bit along the ridge until I got to the edge. With one hand on the roof, I leaned over.

Kat grinned up at me, looking silly from that angle.

I snapped a picture of her and took a couple more photos of the side of the building as I looked down. I leaned out a little more to get one final pic.

Perhaps a little too far out.

My head started to swim, and I almost lost track of which way was up. I started to slip.

"Watch out!" Kat screamed.

I grabbed the edge of the roof with both hands, and the camera slipped out of my hand, tumbling down as I tried to regain my balance. "My camera!" I pushed myself back all the way onto the roof and lay down until the sky stopped spinning around me. I stuck my head over the edge and looked down, dreading what I might see.

"Don't worry." Kat held up my camera with a huge grin on her face.

"You caught it?" I couldn't believe my luck.

"Hey, I wasn't catcher on the softball team for nothing. Have a little faith in me. I'm just glad *you* didn't fall. I don't think I could have managed *that* catch."

I laughed as my muscles got some strength back in them. "I think it's time to come down now. I've had enough roof climbing for one day."

After I made it back to earth, we found a nice grassy spot near the building to rest. We sat for a bit and reviewed the pictures I had taken.

Now that I was safe again, I didn't regret my climb. One or two of the photos might even have a chance. I'd have to see what they looked like on the computer before I knew for sure. Another perspective couldn't be a bad thing. And what was life without a few adventures?

"You realize," Kat said, "that you've left your aunt all alone to set up her stuff in your room, don't you? I wonder if her idea of where things should go is the same as yours."

I sat straight up. "Oh, fur balls. I hadn't thought of that. We'd better get the ladder back and see what damage she's done."

We returned the ladder without being seen and headed to my room. Or, should I say, what *used* to be my room.

I opened the door and gasped. This was *not* going to work.

4

"Oh, hi, JJ," Lissa chirped as I stepped gingerly into the room. "And your mom said your little friend is named Katelyn. Hi, Katelyn."

I looked at Kat and she looked at me.

We both rolled our eyes.

Little friend? That sounded like the kid that came over for a play date in kindergarten. And nobody had called Kat "little" since about fourth grade.

"This is my friend, Kat," I said stiffly. "Kat, this is Melissa, my aunt."

"Just call me Lissa." My aunt smiled and waved her hand about, in the general direction of the mess she had made. "What do you think of my room improvements? I'm not done yet, of course. I'll clean up that stuff soon."

"That stuff" must have meant the boxes and papers scattered over what little bit of the floor could still be seen with all her furniture moved in. The "room improvements" I assumed meant the posters, pictures, and fabrics she had hung around the room. Several wild abstract paintings filled with bright blues, reds, and yellows hung on one wall. Ansel Adams had been replaced by a big photo of some guy I didn't recognize. Instead of Gram's peaceful painting, there was a big painting of randomly scattered black and gray squares.

Ugly, very ugly.

A long, gauzy piece of greenish-blue material hung on a cord that extended across the middle of the room, between our beds. Actually *middle* wasn't quite accurate. It was much closer to my bed than hers.

"What's that for?" I pointed to the fabric.

"That's a room divider," Lissa replied. "For privacy."

"Oh." I looked at Kat, whose expression reminded me of Tasha's in the vet's office. "And who's that guy?" I pointed to Ansel Adams's replacement.

"That's my boyfriend, Thomas." A sad look came over her face. "I thought he was going to move to Oregon with me, but he changed his mind. I'm still trying to convince him. If he loves me, he'll come, don't you think?"

I shrugged. When it came to boys, I didn't have a clue.

"Yeah." Kat pursed her lips and nodded. "That's what always happens in the movies. True love can never be separated by time or space. Of course, that's assuming it's true love."

Lissa frowned. "Of course it is."

Kat nodded again. "Right."

I studied the abstract paintings. Was there anything good in them?

No, not really.

"Could we maybe put some different pictures on the wall?" I spun slowly, taking in the whole room. "Some that actually look like something."

"Oh, those *do* look like something. You just have to use your imagination. Like that one over there." Lissa pointed to the one with the black and gray squares. "That's a commentary on the problem of conformity.

It exposes the banality of life when we all remain confined to our little boxes."

"The bane-what-ity?" Kat's forehead furrowed.

"Banality," Lissa said in a teacher voice. "Triviality, triteness."

Kat still looked confused.

I certainly couldn't help.

Lissa sighed and shook her head. "I guess I can't expect twelve-year-olds to understand these things. Banality is, like, how boring things are."

"Oh." Kat slouched and plopped down onto my bed. "Boring I know about."

"Those pictures are boring," I said. "You took down Ansel Adams for this junk?"

"Well, I like them." Lissa raised an eyebrow.

"Well, I don't, and it's my room." My insides were getting warmer, and it didn't have anything to do with today's weather. "You can put whatever you want there under your bed, but I have to look at the other walls. And I can't stand looking at these." I walked over to that banality picture, lifted it off the nail, carried it over to Lissa's side of the room, and set it down next to her desk.

Lissa stared at me, lips pressed together. She picked up the painting, carried it back across the room, and hung it back on the nail. "You should learn to appreciate art."

"I do appreciate art," I cried, my voice rising. "I love Gram's art. And you took Gram's picture down to put up that stupid, *boring* picture." I looked around the room until I spotted where Lissa had put Gram's painting—leaning against my desk. I removed the box

24

picture and stuck Gram's picture back where it belonged.

"I didn't know that was Grandma's painting." Lissa ran a hand through her hair. "Still, you need to appreciate different styles of art. Not everything has to look real. And I have a right to have some of *my* pictures up. While I'm here, this is my room too."

A knock came from the open door. We both spun toward it.

Mom stood there, a concerned look on her face. "I heard what sounded like arguing. What's the matter?"

Kat looked from me to Lissa and then quietly stood up and backed out into the hall. "I think I'll stay out of this. Be right out here, JJ."

"Aunt Lissa took down Gram's painting and put up some painting of boxes. And she didn't even ask me." I sounded whiny, but I couldn't help it.

Mom looked over at Lissa.

"I was trying to brighten up the room. I'd like to have some of my things on the walls." She sighed. "Why do I suddenly feel like a kid who moved back home after college and can't seem to fit in?"

"Can we compromise?" Mom looked at me.

I snorted. Compromise? Why did I have to compromise in my own room?

Mom gave me a pleading look.

I studied Gram's painting. Gram loved family— more than almost anything. "The first gift God ever gives us is our family," she would tell me. "Which shows how important it is."

Maybe for her. Not so much for me.

Still, maybe I could compromise for a little while.

Lissa wouldn't be here forever, would she? I motioned toward the pictures on Lissa's side of the line. "She can keep those little pictures up, if I can keep Gram's picture up." The words almost got stuck in my throat.

Mom looked back at Lissa.

Lissa shrugged. "I didn't know Grandma painted that picture. I wouldn't mind having something of hers on the wall. That deal would work for me."

Mom smiled. "Good. Now, JJ, can you help me fix dinner?" She stepped out into the hall. "Kat, you may stay for dinner if it's all right with your mom."

Kat nodded. "Okay. Thanks, Mrs. Monroe. "

"And, Lissa, clean up that mess." Mom laughed as she said it, and Lissa laughed too, so everything was all right.

Except that I felt like I was living in someone else's house—or at least someone else's bedroom. *Please get a job soon, Lissa. If you don't, this could end up being the worst summer of my life.*

5

In my dream, rain fell, pattering on the roof and hitting the window. It seemed to stop and start in odd ways.

Gradually, I awoke with the feeling that something wasn't quite right. I opened one eye.

What was that flimsy-looking curtain doing next to my bed? Were we on vacation someplace, staying in an old motel with our luggage crammed into every odd space?

The tapping sound from my dream continued from behind the curtain.

I opened the other eye and propped myself up. Reality smacked me across the face.

Lissa had moved in.

I reached over, lifted the curtain, and peeked underneath.

Lissa sat in gray sweat pants and a purple tank top at the desk under her bed, typing away on her laptop, stopping every so often to look through a pile of papers on the desk.

"What are you doing?" I may have sounded a bit grumpy.

Lissa looked over with a cheerful smile. "Well, good morning, sleepyhead. I'm updating my résumé so I can apply for work."

"Oh. Okay." Résumé? What was that? Oh well. Anything that helped her apply for work must be a good thing. I let the curtain fall and looked at my clock. Ugh. "It's only seven thirty. I like to sleep in during the summer. I shouldn't be waking up at seven thirty until September."

Lissa laughed. "Well, go back to sleep, then. I'll be quiet." She tapped away on the laptop.

I opened the blinds. The sun was shining, and it looked like another beautiful day. I sat up. Morning light was supposed to be the best for taking pictures. "The time of day when heaven lights up the darkness," Gram always said.

Since I was already wide awake, I might as well take advantage of it.

I climbed out of bed, pulled on jeans and a T-shirt, strapped on my watch, and grabbed my camera. Someday I would have a smart phone with a camera and watch all-in-one. Maybe when Mom finished school and got a teaching position, I'd get one. "See you later," I said as I opened the door. "I'm going out to take some pictures."

Lissa smiled at me and went back to her work. Good idea.

I popped into the bathroom, splashed some water on my face, and combed my hair. Ouch. How could shoulder-length hair get so tangled just by sleeping on it?

Guys were lucky. They could have really short hair without anyone thinking they were weird.

Brett was snoring softly as I passed his room. No need to be quiet; it took an earthquake, or a similar force of nature, to wake him. Mom and Dad's voices came from their room, but they'd be getting ready for work, so I stayed out of their way.

In the kitchen, I paused long enough to eat a banana and find a granola bar. If I wanted to catch the good light, I couldn't take time to fix an actual breakfast. A true photographer had to put her art before her stomach.

I did put some food in Tasha's bowl. Art might come before *my* stomach, but it didn't come before the cat's. Finally, I was out the door, looking for prize-winning photo ops.

What would qualify for the landscape category? Did it have to be some beautiful, postcard-worthy scenery, or could it be something smaller? Nothing around here met my definition of landscape. Maybe I could talk Mom or Dad into taking me to Mt. Hood or Multnomah Falls. Or even the beach.

No, that wouldn't work. They were going to the beach by themselves next weekend for their anniversary. They wouldn't want to make another trip right away just for me.

But maybe Multnomah Falls or another waterfall in the Columbia Gorge. We were close enough to drive there and back in an evening. And evening light was almost as good as morning light.

I walked past Kat's house. No use checking. She'd be asleep.

The bigleaf maple tree at the corner might make a good photo. I framed a picture in the viewfinder. A pattern of bright green leaves glowing in the morning sun. Nice. I took a couple extras for good measure. A vine maple, whose branches curved and twisted in graceful patterns, provided the next few shots. The sunlight edged the branches in gold. Nice, again. I even took pictures of a few houses for the building category.

But nothing seemed special enough for the contest. It would take a lot more than a "nice" picture to win the grand prize.

I wandered slowly back home.

Mom's car was backing out as I reached the driveway. She stopped and rolled down the window. "What's up, JJ?" she asked. "Pretty early for you to be out and about."

I grabbed the window frame and leaned in through the opening. "Somebody woke me up. She didn't mean to, but she did. So I thought I would get out and take some pictures for that photo contest I told you about at dinner."

She patted my hand. "That's a great idea. Seize the moment."

"Huh?"

"Never mind. It's something we old folks say. Just don't go too far by yourself." She started to roll the window back up, but I kept my hands on the edge of the glass.

"Mom, I can't get any really good photos around here. Could you take me to the Gorge or Mount Hood? I could get some great landscapes there."

Mom frowned. "I'm awfully busy with work. Plus, I've got homework and a paper due for my class. And you know Dad and I will be gone this coming weekend."

I nodded but tried to look as sad as I could.

Mom laughed. "Sorry. Even your puppy dog face won't help. I don't have time. Why don't you ask your dad? I have to go now."

I stepped back.

She rolled the window up and pulled away.

Should have known. She never had time for me anymore. And chances weren't much better with Dad.

I sat on the back steps and went over the contest categories again: people, animals, landscape, buildings, and sports. I'd worked some on buildings and landscape, although the results weren't great. For people, I always had Kat as a subject. She might not be the most elegant model, but she loved posing. For animals, there was, of course, Tasha. And maybe I could track down a squirrel or two outside, or get close enough to a robin or scrub jay. But sports? When was Brett's next baseball game? Brett liked to pose almost as much as Kat.

A few dark clouds gathered along the edges of the blue sky.

Uh-oh. *That* picture meant rain was coming in. If it rained, I would have to stick to indoor shots.

I checked my watch. 8:30. Kat might be up. I meandered over to her place, keeping my eye open for good moments to capture. Stopping outside Kat's window, I held my breath and listened.

Only silence.

Hmm. Should I risk waking her? I shrugged. Why not? She usually got over her grouchiness pretty fast. I knocked on the window.

No answer.

I tried again, a little harder.

Was that a muffled groan from inside?

"Hey, Kat! Wake up!" I called.

Something banged against the inside of the window.

"Come on. I know you're in there."

The window opened and Kat's shape appeared through the screen. "It's too early. What do you want?"

"There are clouds coming in. I need to get some more pictures while it's still nice out. And I need your help."

She groaned. "Go away and come back in an hour."

"Pleeeeease ..." I whined back. "I need your help."

Kat sighed loudly. "Okay, but no ladders this time."

"All right. We can find other ways to be creative."

Kat pushed the screen out of the window and let it fall to the ground. "Come on in. I'm not awake enough to go open the front door."

I handed her my camera, so it wouldn't get damaged, and pulled myself up to the windowsill. Kat's bed was right on the other side, so I pushed myself forward and landed with a plop on top of the rumpled covers. I righted myself, settled back on the bed next to the open window, and looked at Kat.

Yup, she had definitely been sleeping. She wore her Cinderella nightgown—a gift from a grandma who didn't know her very well—and her hair stuck out in odd directions. Her eyes were kind of halfway open.

She slumped back onto the bed and stuck her feet under the covers piled at the end of the mattress. "We really have to take pictures now?"

"We really do."

"You going to share the prize money with me?" She gave me a sleepy-eyed, hopeful yet suspicious look.

"I'll give you twenty-five percent. I think that's a fair amount."

"A *fair* amount," Kat crowed, with her first hint of

enthusiasm. "A fair amount from the county fair—get it?"

Well, at least she was waking up. I got her moving, and we spent the morning wandering the neighborhood, taking pictures. Kat posed for me in front of trees and buildings. I took one picture from the ground looking up at her and another from a tree looking down, with branches framing her face. She insisted that I take a few of her making weird expressions. Those were definitely not winners, but a photographer had to keep her model happy, so I went along with it.

At eleven o'clock Kat had to go home and get ready for a dentist appointment. I had lots of photos in my camera now. The only question I had was if any of them were good. And how was I supposed to figure that out?

Silly me! Gram was an artist. And I hadn't visited her for over a week. I fixed myself a quick sandwich for lunch and told Lissa where I was going, in case Mom called.

I set off to see Gram.

6

Gram's place was only a mile away and had a bike lane the whole trip, so Mom didn't mind if I rode by myself. As I pedaled along, the sky got darker. Thick gray clouds moved in from the west—the kind of clouds that rolled on during a movie right before something bad happened. Still, they made a nice picture, with the green maples and alders bright against them, even if the clouds would probably bring rain.

I stopped, pulled out my camera, and snapped a couple of pictures. As I put the camera back, I felt around in my backpack.

Yep, my jacket was there, just in case. But maybe the rain would hold off until I got home.

I pulled up in front of Big Maples Retirement Home. It was named for the two maple trees in front, which gave some nice shade in summer and turned all gold and red in the fall. I took a picture of one of them, a picture of the building, and a couple more of the yellow and peach roses blooming near the front door.

I got the clouds again for good measure, locked my bike to the empty bike rack by the door, and walked inside.

"Hi, JJ," the receptionist called out. "I think your great-grandma is down in the game room."

I waved. "Thanks. I'll go find her." I padded along the carpet that smelled faintly of disinfectant. The sound of a TV and old folks' voices came from down the hall. At the far end of the game room, Gram worked on a jigsaw puzzle, her white head bobbing up and down as she searched for pieces and chatted with the dark-haired lady next to her. When she looked in my direction, her face lit up. "JJ, how wonderful to see you!" she called.

The other lady looked over too. She seemed familiar.

"Elsie, you remember my great-granddaughter, JJ, don't you?" Gram asked, smiling at me.

I went over and gave Gram a big hug.

"Of course, Rose, of course. How could I forget her? You talk about her all the time." Elsie wrinkled her nose in a smile.

Eyes twinkling, Gram pushed up from the chair, grabbing her cane to steady herself. "Outside or to my room?"

"Your room, please. I want to show you some pictures I took."

She motioned toward the half-finished puzzle. "Now don't you finish that without me, Elsie."

Elsie winked. "We'll see."

We took the elevator up to Gram's room, #205. Gram leaned on her cane and took slow steps, which was a bit odd. She was usually pretty energetic for being so old.

"Are you feeling okay?"

"I'm fine, dear. Just tired. I didn't sleep too well last night. We old folks have that problem sometimes." After she unlocked the door, she paused for a moment and looked at me. "You have a new houseguest now, don't you?"

35

Nodding, I tried not to frown.

"How's that working out?"

I studied the carpet. "Too soon to tell, I guess. I don't really like sharing my room, but what can I do?"

Gram walked into her apartment and closed the door behind us. "Did I ever tell you that I had to share my room with two sisters? We had our share of fights, but we never got lonely."

I grimaced. Sometimes those "good old days" didn't sound that great. One temporary roommate was bad enough.

"Family is special, Jada Jane. Treasure them while they are here. You never know when they might be gone." A sad, faraway look passed over her face.

Did she still miss Gramps after all these years?

She reached out to touch my hair. "Come on. Let's see those pictures you've got." She led the way to the living room.

On the far wall hung two of Gram's paintings—one of Mt. Hood rising over the trees with flowers in the front part, and the other of a lighthouse high atop an ocean cliff with waves pounding the shore below. The ocean picture always made me want to go to the beach.

Another wall showed off a photograph of Tasha and me. I had used the timer on my camera to take it and had given it to Gram on her last birthday. It looked pretty nice up there on the wall across from her own beautiful paintings.

"Can we sit at the computer?" I asked. "I'm trying to decide which pictures to print and which to erase. There's a photography contest at the county fair, and I want to enter it."

"What a wonderful idea!" Gram rapped her cane a couple of times on the floor. "You should definitely enter. Do they have a separate division for kids?" Gram settled into the chair in front of her computer.

I moved another chair over next to her. "They do, but I want to win the grand prize. It's a new digital SLR camera, a really nice one. I could take great pictures with a camera like that." Oops. I didn't mean to imply that the camera Gram gave me was bad. "Uh, this camera takes good pictures. It just doesn't have manual controls and all that."

Gram laughed. "Oh, I know your present camera leaves a lot to be desired. It's a starter camera, and you're off to a good start."

Whew. Good thing Gram's feelings didn't get hurt easily. I sat down, pulled my camera from the backpack, and attached it to the computer with a cord.

The pictures started loading.

"The most important thing isn't the camera, but the person taking the pictures," Gram said. "It's like any form of art. You have to learn to really see the pictures before you create them. Part of it is a God-given gift, I believe. Part of it can be learned."

"Do you think I have the gift?" What did it feel like to be gifted? So many times I had great ideas for pictures, but they rarely turned out the way I wanted.

"I believe you do, child." She wrapped one arm around me. "Just be sure to use it for God's glory."

"I'm not sure how to do that." Gram talked about God a lot, like they were good friends, special friends. Sometimes it made me kind of ache inside, like when I first stayed at a friend's house overnight and got homesick. Other times it seemed almost scary. Did I really want someone always watching me?

"You'll figure it out. Just listen to His voice. If you open your heart to listen to Him, He can show you how."

The pictures finished loading, and Gram started the slide show, clicking slowly through them. She stopped for a moment when she saw the ones from the school roof. "JJ, what were you doing?" She looked at me with her eyebrows raised.

"Maybe we should skip a few." I showed all my teeth in a corny grin. "You don't have to say anything about these to Mom, do you?"

Gram patted me on the back. "Not if you stay off roofs from now on." Her expression looked serious, but her eyes twinkled.

I grinned. "Okay, I'll stay off roofs. But it *was* kind of fun."

"You be careful. I want my great-granddaughter to outlive me."

We finished the slide show, and Gram told me which ones she liked best. I went through them again on the camera, erasing the ones I didn't like. A few had possibilities, but none really seemed that great.

"Do you think any of those have *Grand Prize* written all over them?" I clicked through them really quickly.

Gram pursed her lips and squinted a bit. "You have talent, JJ. Your photographs are quite good for a twelve-year-old. And a couple of those might win a prize in your age range. But I don't think you have the grand-prize winner yet."

I nodded, shoulders sagging. She was right, of

course, but it would have been nice to get a winner right off the bat.

"Keep working on it, sweetie. I believe in you, and so does God."

"Huh? I thought we were supposed to believe in God, not God believe in us."

Gram smiled that smile that made it seem like she was seeing something no one else could see. "Works both ways, JJ. Works both ways."

Before I left, Gram gave me a few dollars to stop at the camera shop on the way home and order some prints.

"The man there is a true artist," she said, "as well as a very nice man. He'll be glad to help you."

"I'll be back soon, Gram, with more photos." I hugged her. "Maybe a prize winner."

"That's my girl," she said, waving at me as I got on the elevator.

Ray's Camera Shop was in a little building with faded paint and a store front that could use a good washing. The display area inside the front window held a bunch of different cameras, from point-and-shoots to DSLRs. One of the grand-prize models sat in the center, wearing a very high price tag.

I opened the door, and a little bell jangled above me. Inside, the walls were covered with photographs— seascapes and mountains, ferns and butterflies, babies and old men. So many different kinds of pictures, but they were all beautiful. They made me feel like I was seeing things clearly for the first time, like I could walk into the scenes and know exactly what was going on. I stared for a minute or so.

"May I help you, young lady?" a gruff but gentle voice asked. An older man stood behind the counter. He was mostly bald with woolly, white hair around the edges of his head that framed a brown, wrinkled face. His dark eyes sparkled with life. He *did* look like an artist.

"I want to order some photographs. I'm going to enter the county fair contest."

"Wonderful!" he said. "A budding photographer. I'd be happy to help you. My name's Ray Browning." He reached out a hand.

"I'm JJ," I said, shaking his hand. I gave him the memory card, and he put it in his computer. I went through the different pictures, choosing the ones I wanted: a maple tree, a couple of views from the top of the school—including the one of Kat, because I liked it—and one of an old house down our street.

Mr. Browning looked over the pictures with me. "Pretty nice. You have some good ones there. I like the perspective of the roof pictures. And you have a nice balance of colors in the one of the tree." He stepped back and crossed his arms. "You know, I offer photography classes. I have a couple of kids not much older than you signed up. You should think about it."

Photography classes? How neat would that be? To learn how to take pictures like those on the wall. "How much are the classes?" I held my breath.

Mr. Browning handed me a small brochure with classes and prices listed.

My breath came out in a long sigh. Mom was always reminding me how tight money was. She would never spend that much on classes for me. I handed the brochure back. "Maybe sometime."

Mr. Browning wrote down my order, showed me the mats I would need to put the pictures on for the contest, and told me to come back on Friday.

I thanked him and opened the door. A wet, windy blast hit my face. So much for the rain holding off. I pulled out my jacket, put the camera in a plastic bag in the pack, and prepared for a very wet ride home.

7

By the time I got home, I was soaked, despite my coat. Good old Oregon rain. I was getting hungry, which always made me grumpy. *Please, Lissa, have dinner started. I hope you're a good cook. Some fancier meals would be nice.* Mom usually only had time to throw something quick together when she got home. Although she was also encouraging me to try my hand at dinner, now that I was twelve.

I put away my bike and walked in the back door to the yummy smell of chocolate chip cookies and the yucky sight of a big mess. Dirty mixing bowls sat in the sink. The chopping board lay on the counter with little bits of walnut all over it and a knife sitting next to it. The chocolate chip bag was still out, along with half a cube of margarine, a box of brown sugar, the sugar and flour bins, and the greasy cookie sheets. The cookies filled a big plate, though, and they *did* look good.

I grabbed one and started toward the hall.

Wait. Either the TV was going, or we had visitors. I turned toward the family room.

Lissa sat on the couch with her feet up on the coffee table, watching some talk show. "Oh, hi!" she chirped when she saw me. "Have a cookie. I felt like baking."

I took a bite. Mmm. The chocolate chips were still gooey and warm. "But you didn't feel like cleaning up?"

She waved her hand. "I was going to, but this talk

42

show came on, and it's really funny. I can't believe how stupid people can be."

Neither can I. I stared straight at Lissa. But I only said, "Mom will be home in a few minutes. She hates to come home to a messy house."

"Oh, I'll get to it in a bit. This show only goes another half hour."

I glared at her, arms crossed. But she was so intent on her show that she didn't even seem to notice. A loud sigh didn't work either. Was she really that wrapped up in the show, or was she ignoring me on purpose? Finally, I gave up.

I dumped my wet pack in the corner. I had three choices: leave it and have an angry parent, clean it up myself, or get in a fight with Lissa. And I didn't feel like fighting. Nor did I want Mom in a bad mood. That would totally get the evening off on the wrong foot.

As I cleaned, I fumed inside. Lissa made the mess, and she had plenty of time to clean it up. It wasn't fair that I got stuck with it. I washed the bowls and cookie sheets, put away the ingredients, and wiped off the chopping board. I finished as Mom walked in the door.

"Oh, what a wet day it turned into." Water dripped from her hair onto her blouse. "And I didn't think to take an umbrella or coat this morning." She looked me up and down. "It appears you didn't either. You should go put on some dry clothes, JJ."

"I was going to, but Lissa made cookies and left a mess, so I was cleaning up first." Would that be enough to get Lissa in trouble?

Mom smiled.

Apparently not.

"Well, that's really nice of you to clean up for her. And nice of her to make cookies. They look good."

I clomped down the hall to my room to change. Why wouldn't Mom take my side? Did she love her little sister more than me?

At least Lissa hadn't done any more damage to the room. And since she wasn't there at the moment, I could relax. I put on dry clothes and threw my wet stuff into the laundry bin. Then I flopped down on my bed and stared at the ceiling. I left the door open so I could hear if Mom called.

Footsteps tromped down the hall. They stopped outside my room.

There was Brett munching on a cookie, with two more in his other hand. "Hey, JJ. Good cookies, huh?"

I sat up. "I guess so."

Brett looked around the room. "Kinda crowded in here."

"That's for sure."

"Glad it was an aunt and not an uncle." He chuckled.

I scowled at him. "Thanks a lot."

"Sorry. But can you imagine how long it would take to get *my* room clean enough for a visitor?"

He did have a point. But it still wasn't fair.

Brett turned and left.

"Hey, Brett!"

He came back to the doorway.

"When's your next baseball game?"

"I've got an away game Wednesday, if it doesn't get rained out, and a home game Saturday. Why? You aren't getting interested in baseball, are you?" He raised one eyebrow.

I laughed. "Nah, nothing like that. But I need some sports photos for the photography contest I told you about at dinner last night. Could I come along and take pictures?"

He stood a little taller, grinning. "Sure. You can be my paparazzi. Be sure to let me know when the talent scouts start calling."

"Don't worry. You'll be the first to know."

Mom fixed tuna casserole for dinner, along with salad from a bag. I helped by adding some tomatoes and carrots to the salad mix. Lissa was in my bedroom on her computer, supposedly checking on some job leads.

Right. That certainly explained the chat window that was up when I peeked in.

Dad came into the kitchen from work and looked at the tuna casserole. His face drooped a bit. "I thought maybe our guest would make us something good," he grumbled.

"Are you complaining about my tuna casserole?" Mom had a teasing look on her face. She waved a serving spoon at him like a sword.

Dad raised his hands in pretend fear.

I cracked up. So many of my friends' parents weren't together anymore. My parents might be a pain at times, but at least they were both still here.

"Lissa did make some cookies." Mom took another stab at him, this time at his stomach. "So you get dessert tonight."

"Guess that will have to do."

The next morning the pattering I heard as I woke really *was* rain. All I could see outside were water droplets and gray skies and plants sagging under the wetness. No picture-taking expeditions today.

I lifted the silky curtain.

What, Lissa was still sleeping? It was after eight thirty. Weird.

Oh, yeah, she had been watching some movie on TV when I went to bed.

Dad had seemed a bit annoyed—I think he wanted to watch something else, but was too polite to say anything.

The last time Aunt Lissa visited us, I must have been about eight. That time, she stayed a week and slept in the family room. She and Mom went shopping and out to lunch, and they talked and laughed late into the night. And one day, Lissa took me shopping, just the two of us. I felt very grown-up being out with my aunt. She bought me a dress that I wore to church on Easter and, later, to school. She had made me feel special that day. I was really sad when I outgrew the dress.

Now things were different. She crowded my space and added tension to the house without even trying.

But she wasn't totally bad. Maybe I needed to give her more of a chance. Gram was always telling me that, to give people a chance. It was the right thing to do, she said, and sometimes people might surprise me in a good way. She said God had a purpose for everyone, and that we might be part of someone else's purpose too.

Maybe. Still, why couldn't Lissa's purpose be in California—or anywhere but my bedroom?

I slipped out of bed and pulled on my usual jeans and T-shirt. I took my camera and headed out to the family room. Tasha seemed my best hope for photos today. Maybe if I kept an eye on her, she would do something unusual or strike a weird pose, and I could get a grand-prize-winning picture. I could hope, anyway.

Tasha wasn't feeling photogenic. She kept moving when I tried to take her picture. Then she moved into the kitchen and sat in front of her food bowl, meowing in her demanding way.

I finally gave up and fed her. After that, I got a couple of pics of her grooming herself before she slipped behind the couch for a morning nap.

What now? I was still the only one up, except for Mom and Dad, of course, who were long gone. Maybe I should do something nice and fix breakfast for Brett and Lissa. I liked making pancakes, and we hadn't had those for a while. Everybody in the family liked my pancakes. I went into the kitchen and pulled out eggs, milk, flour, oats, and baking powder.

I mixed the batter, added a few frozen blueberries for good measure, and heated the pan.

It was 9:30. Lissa should be up soon. Brett, not so much. For pancakes, he would probably be okay with being rousted from bed.

I set plates and silverware on the table, along with butter and syrup. Then I went back down the hall, looking for hungry people.

Lissa opened one eye when I entered the room.

"Ready for breakfast? I'm making pancakes."

She sat up. "It *is* time to get up, isn't it? Sure, I'll take some pancakes. I hope you have blackberry syrup. Grandma always used to make blackberry syrup when we lived up here."

I shook my head. "No blackberry syrup. But the pancakes have blueberries in them."

"That might work." Lissa still looked a bit disappointed.

I knocked on Brett's door.

A low grunt came from inside.

"Wake up, Brett. Time for breakfast." I waited.

Brett had a bad habit of going back to sleep and having to be reawakened.

"Brett, pancakes."

"Huh?" Movement, rustles of covers, and squeaks from the bed. "Pancakes?"

"I'm making pancakes. They'll be ready in five minutes."

"Oh, okay. Kind of early, though."

I went back to the kitchen and poured the batter into round blobs in the pan. The blobs spread out until they almost touched, the blueberries adding little blue bumps to them. I watched carefully, flipping the pancakes when they were all bubbly.

Lissa walked into the kitchen and plopped down at the table.

Brett showed up as I took the pancakes from the pan. He looked at least half awake. "Ah, your special pancakes. Nice," he mumbled, before digging in.

I cooked some more, while Brett and Lissa ate the first batch.

"Not bad," Lissa said. "They'd be better with blackberry syrup, though. And what's the crunchy stuff in them?"

"Oatmeal," I said. "I like oatmeal in my pancakes."

"Is there whole wheat flour in there?" A wary look came over her face.

"Some. Is that a problem?"

"I'm more a white flour person myself. But they're not bad."

Rolling my eyes, I turned away. *Some people.* If I gave her a hundred dollars, would she complain it wasn't in the right denominations?

"I think they're great, JJ. Thanks," Brett said. "Your pancakes are worth getting up early for."

"It's not really that early." I pointed at the clock.

"You just say that 'cause you're not a teenager yet. I'm a growing boy, and I need my sleep. And my food." He put a couple more pancakes on his plate and drowned them in syrup.

After breakfast, Brett went to get ready for his summer job at the local hamburger place.

Lissa started back toward our room.

"Hey," I called. "Aren't you forgetting something?"

Lissa turned and squinted at me, her eyebrows all squished together. "Forgetting something? What? Was I supposed to say 'thank you'? Well then, thank you."

"No, that's not it." Heat rose in my face. "How about cleaning up the kitchen? I cleaned up your mess from the cookies last night. And my mess is a lot smaller than that."

Lissa looked at her watch. "Sorry. I need to check on some jobs. I might be able to get in for an interview this morning. Maybe next time." She smiled and slipped into the bedroom.

What an ungrateful jerk! I tried to do something nice for her, and not only did she complain about the food, but she wouldn't even help clean up. I wanted to break something. The phone rang and I answered.

"I'm bored," Kat said. "Can I come over?"

My anger drained away. Kat could make anything fun. "Sure, if you don't mind helping me clean up the kitchen."

8

"We need to think of something exciting to do." Kat finished wiping out the frying pan. "A rainy day doesn't have to be boring."

"So, what will it be? Give the cat a bath, or lock Lissa in the bedroom?" I'd never tried giving Tasha a bath, but given the way she usually reacted around water, it would definitely be a dangerous venture. Locking Lissa in sounded like more fun. Naughty, maybe, but fun.

Kat's eyes narrowed. "Ah, but you aren't thinking outside the box yet. There are always more than two options. Though that second one does sound pretty nice."

Brett rushed into the kitchen, glanced at the clock, grabbed a banana off the counter, and banged out the back door. Late again. Good thing his boss liked him.

"Your brother makes things exciting. Like everything's a race. But we don't have anywhere to race to."

Lissa came down the hall, dressed in a dark blue skirt, white blouse, and those high heels of hers, carrying a rain coat. "Got an interview." She pranced out the door, pulling the coat over her as the screen door closed behind her.

Of course, she forgot to close the other door.

I slammed it shut. *Did you hear that, Lissa? Maybe you*

could close it yourself next time.

Her car roared to life and backed out of the driveway.

"Yes! We're alone." I thrust both arms up in the air. "Now we can sing and dance and make all the noise we want."

"Rah, rah, rah!" Kat yelled, dancing around the room, arms swinging wildly until one arm slammed into the counter. "Ouch!" She stopped and rubbed the sore spot. "So much for dancing. Maybe we should watch TV."

"Boring. There's got to be something better."

Kat frowned and stared into space, then her eyes got big. "How much do you know about your aunt?"

"What do you mean?"

"She's gone for a while." Kat tapped all her fingertips together like an evil scientist. "We could do some exploring. See if she's hiding any secrets. That's how Mom found out about Dad's girlfriend." Her smile faded. "Well, maybe that's not a good example."

"Lissa would be really mad if she caught us." I frowned. But only a little.

"She won't find out. Come on." Kat ran down the hall.

Scalp tingling a warning, I followed after her. This was not a good idea. But when Kat got something in her head, she didn't let go. Maybe if we looked a little bit, she would be satisfied. And I *was* a bit curious. Who knew? Maybe it would even help me understand Lissa a little better.

Right. Who was I fooling with that lame excuse?

"Keep watch at the door, in case she forgot

something and comes home," Kat said.

I nodded and leaned uneasily against the door frame.

"The desk is a good place to start." She opened the middle drawer. "Pencils, pens, paper clips, stamps … and a picture of her and some guy."

"Same guy as the one on the wall?"

Kat looked up, then back at the picture. "Yeah."

"That's no new information." My brain whispered at me to stop Kat, but I ignored it.

Kat explored the next drawer. "Nothing much here." She sounded disappointed.

"Well, maybe we should find something else to do." I looked toward the back door, but all was quiet.

Kat scrunched up her face for a moment, then smiled. "The computer. She probably has all the good stuff on her computer." She sat down at the desk and moved the mouse.

The screen lit up.

My stomach tightened, and the pancakes in there felt as if they'd turned to stones. But I kept seeing that picture in my head, the one of our whole family smiling—and no Lissa anywhere. Could there be something on her computer that would show me a way to get rid of her?

Kat clicked on different folders.

"What are you looking for, anyway?"

Kat shrugged with her hands out, palms up, eyebrows raised. "I'll know when I find it." She sat up straight. "Email. That's the place to look. Saved email."

"Really?" Wasn't that kind of like reading her diary?

"Yuck. A gooey, gushy one from her boyfriend. Oh, he loves her *so* much. Isn't that *sweet?*" She made kissing sounds. "Kissie, kissie, lovey-dovey."

I laughed at Kat's silly expressions but still felt squirmy. A board in the hallway squeaked, and I about jumped a mile. I whipped my head around.

Whew, just Tasha.

I took a deep breath. "Hurry up."

Kat clicked once more. "Business stuff. Boring."

Another click.

Kat stared at the screen for a long minute, then turned toward me, eyes huge. "Did she tell you why she left her job in California?"

"Not really. She just said that she missed Oregon."

"Maybe, but that's not all."

"What do you mean?"

"She got fired."

"Fired?" I stared at her. "You mean laid off?"

Kat shook her head. "Oh no. It's definitely fired. And they wanted her gone right away. She must have done something pretty awful.

9

Leaving the doorway unguarded, I rushed over to the computer and leaned in close to Kat. "Where does it say Lissa was fired? Does it say why?"

Kat slid off the chair and let me sit down.

The email said Lissa was being let go and that she already knew the reason. She had until the end of the day to clean out her desk and be gone.

That wasn't much notice. I looked at Kat. "It doesn't say why. Maybe she was laid off."

"It says let go. That means fired."

"But what could she have done to be fired? It must have been pretty bad if they only gave her that day to get out. She had a good job. That's what Mom said, anyway."

"Weird. Really weird."

"I've seen enough." I clicked out of the email and stood up. "Is everything just like it was before? We can't let her find out we were snooping."

Kat moved the mouse over a bit and nodded.

"Let's go."

"We could try to find out why she was fired." Kat moved toward the keyboard again.

"No. That's enough. I already know more than I wanted to." I headed for the door. "Let's go bathe the cat or something." Lissa fired? It was hard to believe. Mom said she was smart, and Lissa didn't seem really mean and nasty or anything—just annoying. And sometimes rude. So what would she have been fired for?

Had she goofed off on the job too much? She did seem a bit lazy, judging from the way she avoided cleaning up the kitchen. Or maybe she forgot to do something important and lost money for the company? Or ... I hated to think of it, but what if she had done something really bad—like stealing from the company or lying to the boss? What if she was a criminal running from the law? Did that make us accessories to the crime?

Kat followed me out to the family room. "Whatcha gonna do now? You can't just forget it. Who knows what she did." Kat stared at me, big eyes rimmed with black eyeliner. "Maybe she killed someone."

I rolled my eyes and shook my head. "You don't only get fired for killing someone. You get arrested and put in jail."

"Well ..." Kat's mind seemed to work at trying to come up with some logical scenario. "Okay, she probably didn't kill anybody. But she could have stolen something. Or embezzled—isn't that kind of like stealing too?" She looked a bit confused.

"Yeah, embezzling is stealing money from the company. But if she did that, why would she be living here with us? She could afford a place by herself."

Kat pursed her lips and lifted her hands. "Well, she must have done *something*."

"I wish I knew what." I collapsed onto the couch.

"You need to find out. We should look through her email some more. Maybe we'll find something."

"No." I stared at the floor. "She could come home anytime. What if she caught us?"

"Maybe she'd kill us too," Kat said in a low, spooky voice.

I grabbed a pillow from the couch and threw it at her. "She didn't kill anyone."

Kat grabbed another pillow and whacked me with it, then I hit her with a sofa cushion, and soon every pillow in the room became ammunition in the best pillow fight I'd had in a long time. When one cushion banged against the floor lamp and almost brought it crashing down, we flopped onto the floor, laughing so hard we could barely breathe.

The kitchen door slammed shut, and our laughter faded into out-of-breath panting.

Lissa walked in, glanced over, and stopped in her tracks. "What have you been doing?" she asked, her voice rising and sounding suspiciously like Mom's did in similar situations. "This room looks like a dozen monkeys were let loose in it."

Hadn't she ever seen a room after a pillow fight?

"Ooh, ooh," Kat hooted, pretending to scratch under her arms.

I cracked up again, rolling around on the floor.

"You guys are really strange. Crazy strange." Lissa turned and headed for the bedroom.

I looked at Kat, who made another monkey face.

We both broke into laughter again. Finally, we settled down to normal, more or less, and got busy cleaning up the room—cushions back on the couch, pillows neatly set in the corners of the couch and chair, and everything that had been knocked down picked back up. The room looked as good as new, and Mom would never know.

Unless someone told. Oops. Lissa might be a tattletale.

Kat went home to get some lunch and be ready when her mom called from work to check on her. I went to see what my roommate was up to.

Why had she been fired, anyway? I grinned to myself. Could I use the reason to get her out of the house? If she was some kind of criminal, Mom wouldn't want her rooming with me, would she? But how could I find out without giving away what we'd been doing?

Lissa was sitting at her computer when I walked into the room. She glanced over, face expressionless.

Not a good sign. Did she suspect something? I crossed my fingers behind my back. "Hey," I said, trying to sound cheerful. "How was the job interview?"

"It stunk." Lissa, now back in jeans and a tank top, stared at the computer screen, mouth turned downward in an exaggerated frown.

"You didn't get the job?" Oh, fur and claws. That would have been a quick and easy solution to my problem.

"They didn't say, but I could tell. I won't be hearing from them again. And it was a nice company, a lot like the one I used to work for."

Ah, my opening. "Why did you leave that job? If you liked it so much and all, I mean." I sat down in my chair and smiled at Lissa, playing it cool.

"I wanted to come back to Oregon. I grew up here, and it seems more like home."

"But you said you liked that job. Wasn't it difficult to leave it?"

Lissa gave me a hard look. Uh-oh. Was she getting suspicious? "Not really. I figured I could find a good job up here."

"But you had a boyfriend down there. Don't you miss him?"

Her eyes narrowed. "Why do you care so much? It really isn't any of your business, is it? I wanted to move up here, so I did. Sorry about taking up part of your precious room, but I'll be out as soon as I can. Okay?"

I jerked back. She didn't have to get nasty. But I also felt a bit sorry for her. I hadn't ever been fired, but I had been chosen last for soccer in P.E. and rejection was hard to take. "I didn't mean to make you mad," I said. "I just wondered."

"Well, you can leave me alone," she growled. "I've got jobs to apply for." She turned her back on me.

I stuck my tongue out at her, knowing she couldn't see. *Take that, Lissa.* Now, if I could find out why she got fired.

10

That night I asked Dad if he could take me to some waterfalls in the Columbia Gorge later in the week, so I could take pictures. His answer was pretty much the same as Mom's, except without the homework excuse—he was too busy, he had to get ready for the weekend trip with Mom, and he had chores to do.

But he didn't seem that busy stretched out on the couch, staring at some baseball game on TV. He could find time to go to Brett's games but not to help me win a new camera.

The next morning it rained a little and then cleared up. Clouds drifted across the sky in constantly changing patterns of gray and white. If only the contest had a cloud category.

Clouds were so amazing—the shapes and the shadows and the way light broke through the grayness in long streams, like light from heaven. Gram said that was God smiling down at us. God smiling down at Gram I could see, but smiling at me? Eh, not so much.

Kat came over to help me in the afternoon. We tried to get a good picture of Tasha. I put her in the laundry basket, but she wouldn't settle down and kept turning her back on me when I tried to snap the shutter. Next, I brought out her mouse on a string. Kat pulled it back and forth, so I could try for a good action shot, but Tasha wouldn't cooperate.

She batted at the mouse once, rolled over on her back, and stretched out in a pose that wasn't a bit photogenic.

Finally, I had Kat hold Tasha, thinking I could do the people and animal categories both at once, killing two cats with one stone, so to speak.

By this time, Tasha was getting annoyed with so much unwanted attention. She laid her ears back and growled until Kat put her down.

It was hopeless. We looked at the photos on the camera afterwards, but none of them were much good.

"What am I going to do? I only have a week to get some good pictures if I'm going to have time to get them printed and matted. And nothing seems to be working. That stupid cat isn't helping any."

"Let's work on people instead. I guarantee I'll be a more willing subject than that feline." She grinned. "How about some outdoor shots?" She lowered her voice. "We can talk, you know, about somebody."

We headed out, looking for a good background. Once we got away from the house, Kat turned toward me. "So, have you found out anything else about Lissa?"

"I tried asking her about her work and such, but she started getting suspicious so I had to stop."

"Maybe she's getting suspicious because there's something to be suspicious *of*." Kat lifted one eyebrow.

"Maybe." I nodded. "She didn't seem to like me asking questions. Of course, it could be because the job interview didn't go well."

"And *why* didn't it go well?" Kat raised both eyebrows this time. "Maybe because they wanted to know about her last job ... and she wouldn't talk."

61

"I don't know." Why couldn't Lissa have stayed in California instead of complicating my life? Mom said Lissa was a good person, but ... Other than making cookies, she had still managed to avoid all kitchen chores. She always seemed to leave for her—actually *our*—room right after every meal.

Dad had frowned and looked at Mom after dinner last night, but Mom shook her head at him.

"Let's try some pictures by those roses."

Kat obligingly moved in front of the flowers.

I snapped a couple of pictures. But it seemed so ordinary. There had to be something more original. We walked some more. "A photograph needs to do more than show what's on the outside. I read that in a photography magazine. It said a good photograph shows inner character, not just outer beauty."

Kat tilted her head first to the right and then to the left. "Okay, so what does that mean?"

"It means that a good picture of you should show what you are really like."

"And how can you do that?"

"That's what I'm trying to figure out. Let's go over to the school." We turned around and headed back toward home, drifting across the street and onto the playground.

"So you're saying my true character is a kid in primary school?" Kat asked. She ran to the swings and jumped onto one. "Lookie, Mommy. I can swing real high! I can pump all by myself!"

I laughed and ran over. "Yes, that's the real you. Somebody who loves to act crazy." I snapped pictures of her swinging and making faces at me. I had to jump out of the way once, when she kicked a bunch of bark dust in my direction.

After that we moved on to the climbing area and the slide. I kept running after her, stopping to snap a picture whenever I could.

Kat staring down at me from the top of a wooden "castle." Kat peering through the bars of a bridge. Kat sticking her tongue out as she went down the slide. We finally dropped back into the swings to rest.

"Well, I don't know if I got any good ones, but that was fun. You're really talented at acting crazy."

"Someday I'm going to be a famous actress," Kat said, lifting her nose up in the air, "so I have to practice now."

What could I do but laugh?

I was back in my room, sprawled on my bed, when it started getting close to dinnertime.

Lissa tapped away on her computer.

"Mom will be home before too long." Would she catch the hint? "It might be good to get some dinner started."

"That's a good idea."

My hopes rose.

Lissa stretched. "What are you planning to make?"

A whole load of grumpiness dumped on top of me. I was trying to be nice to her, but this was ridiculous.

"I thought *you* might have some ideas." Could my hints be any stronger?

"Not really. Whatever you like is fine with me." She

didn't even look up from the screen.

So, once again, I was faced with the same problem—should I leave dinner for Mom to do and hope she would get Lissa helping, take the chance Mom would fix dinner herself and be extra tired, or do it myself and have Mom smiling when she walked in the door? If I wanted the slightest chance of Mom driving me anywhere to take pictures, I couldn't have her tired out. I jumped off the bed, stomped to the door, and slammed it on the way out.

Had Lissa noticed? Probably not.

I really wasn't much of a cook, but I could handle spaghetti. I got out the pasta, a jar of sauce, and mushrooms I could cut up and sauté to add to the sauce, and pulled out a package of salad mix. That should make a decent dinner. There might even be a loaf of French bread in the freezer I could add. Maybe it would make Mom and Dad happy enough that they would take me to the Gorge the next day. I really needed some good landscape pictures.

When Mom walked in the door, the sauce was simmering, and water for the pasta was nearly boiling. Her face broke into a big smile. "What a nice surprise. This will give me time to get changed and work on that paper." She came over and hugged me from behind. "Thank you, JJ. I really appreciate your help."

A warm glow lit me up inside. It always made the work feel worthwhile when I made Mom happy. I cut up the French bread and cooked the pasta, humming to myself and thinking about ways to arrange food to make good pictures. A pile of spaghetti with sauce dribbling down and a piece of bread to the side, perhaps. Or a close-up of different vegetables in a salad. Maybe next year the fair would have a food photo category. If so, I would be ready.

I was draining the spaghetti when Dad walked in. "Oh, yum. Smells like an Italian restaurant."

"Thanks, Dad." I puffed up a teeny bit.

He started down the hall, then turned back toward me. "Did Lissa help at all?"

I shook my head.

Dad frowned. "Well, thanks for fixing dinner, JJ. I'll be out in a couple of minutes." And he headed down the hall.

I put everything on the table and took a quick trip to the bathroom.

Voices drifted from Mom and Dad's room.

What were they talking about? Was that my name? I bent my head close to the door, ready to scoot if I heard footsteps coming toward it.

"She's been here four days and just hides back in the bedroom," Dad said. "Couldn't she help cook or something?"

"She made cookies."

Dad again, his voice a bit louder. "That was nice, but she's getting free room and board. You'd think she would clean the bathroom or fix meals. Or at least wash the dishes after dinner."

"Give her time," Mom said quietly. "I'm sure she'll help out more when she gets comfortable here."

"Comfortable?" Dad's voice was really rising now. "I don't think I want her getting comfortable. Too comfortable and she won't want to leave. We can't afford to support her forever."

Now Mom's voice got a bit snippy. "It won't be forever. Just a little bit. She's looking for work." After a moment she continued, so softly I could barely hear. "Please be patient for a little while, Rick. It'll be okay."

Silence for a bit.

Were they hugging or staring coldly at each other?

Dad's voice, softer. "Okay, I'll do my best. But I think she can clean up after dinner tonight."

Time to move on, before someone opened the door. I hated it when Mom and Dad argued. At least they never fought in front of me. In fact, their fights were usually pretty mild.

Not like the way Kat's parents used to fight before the divorce.

Still, it made me shiver a bit. As I passed my room, I knocked on the door. "Dinner."

A muffled answer came from inside.

Brett got home from work just as we sat down to eat, and he brought his appetite. Good thing I had made plenty. Mom and Dad were all smiles at dinner, so maybe it was a hug I heard—or didn't hear. I relaxed a bit. Mom always said meals tasted better when she didn't have to cook them, but I thought they tasted better when I *did* cook them. Maybe the difference was that, to Mom, cooking dinner was an everyday thing, but for me, it was something special.

"Thanks for dinner, JJ." Lissa stood up and took her plate into the kitchen and put it in the dishwasher.

Dad took another bite of French bread, but his eyes never left Lissa. When Lissa started toward the hall, Dad glanced over at Mom.

Mom nodded.

"Lissa," Dad said. "Since JJ fixed us this delicious meal, it doesn't seem right for her to have to clean up after it. Would you mind helping out?"

Lissa looked surprised, almost annoyed, but she quickly put a smile on her face. "Sure. I could clean up. It's just that I don't know where everything goes."

"Leave anything out you're not sure of. I'll put those things away," Mom said.

Lissa smiled like an actress in a movie but not quite as believably. "Okay, thanks."

Dad winked at Mom, who raised her eyebrows in return.

Brett got a confused look on his face.

As his eyes darted back and forth between Mom and Dad, I smothered a laugh and choked a bit on my last sip of milk.

We all left to watch Jeopardy in the family room while Lissa cleaned up.

It seemed to be a good time to give the waterfalls-in-the-Gorge idea another try.

"Mom, Dad? Is there any chance one of you might have time to take me to the Gorge tomorrow? I know you're busy, but I really need to get some good landscape pictures." I put on my best smile. "Please?"

Mom looked at Dad, and he looked back at her.

They both looked at me.

"I'm really sorry, JJ." Mom grimaced. "I have too much work to do. That paper is due next week, and there's a test Monday. After the term ends, I would love to drive you around to take pictures."

"But that'll be too late." A whine slipped into my voice. "The contest is a week from Friday."

"Rick?" Mom looked over at Dad.

Dad shook his head. "You need to give us more warning, JJ. I have a lot to do this week."

"I couldn't give you more warning. I only found out about the contest on Sunday. How am I going to get an awesome photograph if I'm stuck here at home?" I stood up, still pleading with my eyes.

But Mom and Dad shook their heads again.

"Brett?" I was getting desperate.

"I've got work and baseball practice. Sorry."

I slumped down into the couch. Now what was I supposed to do?

No use hanging out here.

I stomped down the hall to take a shower.

11

The next morning I lay in bed for a long time. There were no more pictures worth taking in the neighborhood, and nobody would drive me anywhere. What was the point in waking up?

Lissa got out of bed and went straight to tapping away at her computer.

Was she applying for jobs or sending messages to her friends?

After a while she stuck her head around the curtain. "Hey, sleepyhead, why are you lying in bed on such a nice day? I would think you'd be outside taking pictures."

Humph. She seemed awfully happy today. "Why should I get up? Nobody will take me anywhere that I can get good photos." I stared at the boring, white ceiling.

"Where do you want to go?"

"The Gorge. I'd like to get some waterfall pictures for the landscape category."

"Really?" She twirled a piece of hair around her finger. "I haven't been to the Gorge for years. I used to go hiking there a lot when I lived in Portland."

I turned toward her, a glimmer of hope rising inside. "Will you take me?"

She smiled. "Why not? I already put in applications for a couple of jobs this morning, so I deserve a break, right?"

I bolted upright. "Definitely." I studied her face. "You're not joking, are you? You'll really take me?"

"Sure, I'll take you. Why don't you get dressed and fix us some sandwiches to take along? I'll see if I can find my hiking shoes."

Yeah. Her usual high heels would *not* work for hiking. I jumped out of bed and pulled on my jeans and shirt. Of course, she was having me make the lunch. But that seemed only right, since she would do the driving. I downed a bowl of cereal while making the tuna sandwiches. A bag of potato chips and a couple of water bottles joined them in a paper bag, and I was ready to go—once I got my camera, of course. Couldn't forget that.

The sun sparkled through the trees as we drove toward the Gorge. The sky was summer blue, and the trees glowed in different shades of green. In my mind I took photos as we drove along, practicing for when we got there.

A maple tree we passed had a nice shape. And the day's puffy, white clouds looked especially bright above the old, red barn.

Too bad we weren't going slow enough for me to actually get the pics.

An old man held a little boy's hand and smiled down at him as they walked along the road. That would make a wonderful people picture. It made me think of my family—Gram, my grandparents in California, my other grandpa in Florida. And of course, Aunt Lissa. Lissa didn't seem so bad today. Maybe I would even add her to my mental family picture. Maybe.

I looked over at her. "Did you and Mom play together a lot when you were kids?"

She laughed. "I think your mom babysat me more than she played with me. With her being ten years older, we didn't have a lot in common. I was just the little brat who got into her stuff."

I tried to imagine Mom as a teenager, babysitting Lissa. That picture wouldn't form in my head. The little brat part? Yeah, that was easy.

"But did you get along? Brett and I do pretty well, but sometimes he can be a pain. And some of my friends are always fighting with their sisters."

Lissa pressed the brakes as we swept around a curve. "I guess we got along all right. I looked up to her, and she thought I was a cute baby sister."

"She still calls you her baby sister."

"Once a baby sister, always a baby sister." Lissa chuckled.

We neared Crown Point, a high place at the start of the Gorge with a neat old visitor's center overlooking the Columbia River. The building was made of rock and seemed to fit well with the landscape.

"Can we stop for a sec?" I asked. "I could get some building pics—and landscape too. There's a great view."

"I know." Lissa pulled the car over into the parking area. "Remember, I grew up around here too."

She got out and wandered along the overlook while I snapped a few photos. The sun warmed my back as I watched the sparkling Columbia flow peacefully through the valley below. The gray-brown cliffs, green trees, and deep blue sky made a wonderful picture. I took some of Vista House—the visitor's center. The texture of the rough stone walls on the outside contrasted with the marble walls and arching dome of a ceiling inside. Very nice.

Then we were back in the car, winding down into the Gorge curve by curve. Graceful maples shaded the road and ferns clung to the hillsides. Sunlight glimmered through the trees, making beautiful patterns of light and dark that shifted with the breeze.

"Where do you want to stop?" Lissa asked.

"At the first waterfall. I looked them up on Google. The first one will be Latourell Falls. It'll be coming up soon." I squeezed my camera in my hands and glanced at Lissa. Maybe Kat and I had been wrong about her being fired. Maybe we misunderstood something. She seemed too nice to have done anything that bad.

Well … at least today she did.

Once Lissa pulled into the parking lot, we dashed across the street to where the falls crashed down upon the rocks, sending a misty spray up into the air.

I got some pictures from close to the road, but I wanted one through the trees. "Can we walk up the trail a bit?"

Lissa led the way to the trailhead. "Sure. After all, that's why I put on my hiking boots."

After walking up the trail for a few minutes, I found a good viewpoint. I took a couple of shots of the falls framed by leafy branches, then zoomed in to get a closer view.

We headed back to the car and buckled up.

I bounced my legs as we drove. "Bridal Veil Falls is next. It's a short hike to the falls. Is that okay?"

"Absolutely. Maybe after that one, we can take a

break and eat lunch."

"My stomach likes that idea."

Lissa seemed to be enjoying the beauty of the Gorge as much as I was. As we walked to the fall, bigleaf maples towered above us, mixed with a few fir trees. Lacy ferns grew next to the creek, along with wildflowers of different kinds—white ones, yellow ones, a pretty, pink wild rose.

When I won that fancy camera, I could take flower close-ups. I'd learn all their names and be able to label them correctly.

We came down to the creek and hiked along it toward the falls, where I took more pictures. The creek bubbled over rounded gray rocks, chattering its way through the greenery toward the Columbia River. So peaceful. I drew in a big breath of fresh air.

I crouched down to get a different angle of the creek. Then I stepped out onto a rock in the creek. And onto another one. Halfway across, I stopped to take more photos. I was getting some different viewpoints, which should help in the contest.

Lissa, who had walked ahead on the trail, looked back. She grinned and stepped out onto the rocks herself. She looked almost like a kid, with her arms held out for balance, hopping from rock to rock, her long, blonde hair shining in the sunlight.

I snapped a picture. I could label it *Joy* or *Like a Child*.

I framed another shot of her with the falls in the background. As I watched through the viewfinder, she slipped on a rock and went flying, arms flailing.

My mouth dropped open, even as my shutter finger

kept clicking. After all, a true photographer never misses a good shot. I got one of her crashing into the creek with a big splash, another of her floundering back to her feet, and a last one of her pointing at me and screaming, "Put that camera away!"

Uh-oh.

"Are you okay?" I asked, a little too late to seem sincere.

She glared at me. "You took a picture of me all soaking wet?"

"Uh, well …" I stepped carefully back out of the creek, not wanting to end up like Lissa.

She strode toward me, dripping water as she came. "Give me that camera. I'm erasing your pictures."

I cradled it to my chest. "No. You can't have my camera."

A couple of teenagers were staring at us. They smirked, as if trying not to laugh.

Lissa looked toward them and then snapped her gaze back to me and motioned up the trail toward the car.

I ran back the way we had come, keeping ahead of her. No way would I hand my camera over. Who knew what she would do to it?

By the time we reached the car, Lissa seemed to have calmed down a little bit. At least she wasn't screaming anymore.

I hugged my camera tightly. She really did look funny with her hair dripping wet and maybe a bit muddy in back. But I didn't dare laugh.

"Okay, I won't take your camera if you erase that picture of me."

That picture? She thought I only took one photo of her. Nice. This was working out better than expected. "Okay, okay, I'll erase that picture." I switched the camera to review mode and erased the last picture I had taken. "There. It's gone."

She seemed satisfied and tromped around to the driver's seat. "Okay, get in the car. We're going home."

I slid into the car and fastened my seat belt. "I thought you wanted to have lunch here."

She glared at me. "Right. I love to picnic in soaking wet clothes. Doesn't everyone?"

I sighed. "I suppose this means we can't go to Wahkeenah Falls now. Or Multnomah Falls."

"You got it." She started up the car and turned it toward home.

I slumped in my seat. I hadn't gotten nearly the number of pictures I had hoped for, but I couldn't blame her for wanting to go home. She looked pretty miserable. At least I had gotten a few pictures.

Hopefully they would be worth the trouble.

12

Clouds had returned by the next morning. But who cared? I would get my pictures back from the camera shop today *and* turn in a few more. A couple of nice waterfall shots, a silly one of Kat, and, of course, a great shot of Lissa in the water. I couldn't let her see that one, or it might end up in shreds.

I fed Tasha and cuddled her a bit, until she started squirming and I had to set her down. She stalked away to the family room, probably to sleep. She used to sleep in my room a lot, but it must be too crowded for her now.

I ate a bowl of cereal and cleared off the kitchen table while waiting for ten o'clock to arrive—the time the camera shop opened.

Brett wandered into the room with his usual sleepy morning look.

"What's up?"

"Nothing much. I work a few hours and then have baseball practice. We didn't do so great yesterday, so Coach will probably have us do lots of fielding and base running." He frowned.

"Sounds like fun!" I grinned at him.

Brett put his hands around my neck. His eyes narrowed, and he bared his teeth, looking as mad as he could without actually being mad. "Shut your trap, twerp."

After he let go, I coughed and held my throat, bending over like I was in pain.

"Good try, but I'm not buying it."

I stood up and stuck my tongue out. "Okay. Never mind."

The clock read *9:55.*

All right. Time to get my photos. "Would you let Lissa know I'm going to pick up my photos and visit Gram?"

"Sure. Tell Gram hi for me." He took a bowl out of the cupboard. "Ask her if she'd like to come to my game tomorrow. We could pick her up."

"That'd be fun. I hope she does." I grabbed my pack, put a few dollars in my pocket to pay the camera shop man, and headed out to get my bike.

The clouds looked thin, like a delicate sheet of gray, the kind of clouds that usually clear up by afternoon. Good. Gram probably wouldn't come to Brett's game if it ended up cool or wet, but on a warm, clear day, the chances were better. She *did* like to watch Brett play.

I pulled up at the camera shop, chained my bike to a lamppost, and pushed open the door.

Mr. Browning stood behind the counter, smiling at me. "Hello. And how are you this fine morning?"

"Great. I'm here to pick up my prints." I handed him the receipt.

He opened a large drawer that ran along the wall behind the counter and took out a big envelope. "Here you go, miss. I hope they turned out like you wanted."

I pulled the pictures out of the envelope and gave each a critical look.

Not bad. Though I liked them, I didn't think any of

them were good enough for the grand prize. Still, maybe they could win me first or second place in their categories.

"Thank you. They look good, but I need to order some more." I handed him the memory card from my camera, and he slipped it into the photo-ordering machine. I went through all the pictures I had taken, pointing out the prints I wanted.

"Nice ones," Mr. Browning said. "I like the one of the lady in the water. That expression is, as they say, priceless." He chuckled deep in his throat. "You might add that one of Crown Point. You have a nice angle there."

"If you think it's good enough."

"The composition is different. In a good way." He looked at me. "Have you thought about that photography class? You could really benefit from it. Plus, you'd meet some other kids who are into photography."

"I don't think we can afford it. Maybe I could put it on my Christmas list or something." Photography class. The thought made me feel like I hadn't eaten all day and was watching someone chomp on a pizza. Someday. Maybe someday.

He reached across the counter and handed me a piece of paper. "Well, here's my card, if you change your mind. I'd love to have you come."

I stuck the card in the envelope with the pictures, and placed the envelope carefully in my pack. I put the memory card back in the camera. "Thank you."

"These will be ready Tuesday. I look forward to seeing you then."

I pedaled on to Gram's as the sky gradually brightened. It might clear up sooner than noon.

The lady at the front desk waved at me as I entered. "Hi, JJ. I haven't seen your great-grandma yet this morning. She's probably still in her room."

"Okay. Thanks." I took the elevator up to Gram's floor, walked to the room, and rang the doorbell.

"Just a minute." Her voice came from deep within.

I waited. Some days Gram walked slower than other days—apparently today was one of the slow ones.

The door finally opened, and Gram peered out, leaning on her cane with one hand. "JJ, how nice to see you! Come on in." She stood a bit straighter and her face lit up.

"I have some pictures to show you." I led the way to her living room. "I came straight from the camera shop where I ordered some new pictures. I'll show them to you on the computer."

"Wonderful." She sank down onto the chair in front of the monitor. "I'll sit here, so I don't have to move." She winked one eye at me.

I gave her a hug, and she hugged back with one arm. I closed my eyes for a moment to drink in the smell of lavender perfume and the warmth of her next to me. When she let go, I opened my eyes and pulled the photographs out of the envelope. "Look at these, Gram. What do you think?"

She took her time looking them over, holding them at different angles and squinting to see them better. "Very nice. That one of the maple tree makes me want to sit down against it and enjoy the sunshine."

I grinned. "They came out all right, I think. But I

79

still don't think any of them are grand-prize winners. Do you?" Hope filled the question. Maybe she would see something in the photos that I didn't.

"A category winner, perhaps."

"But no grand prize yet?" I sighed.

"Have faith, and keep on taking pictures. Remember, God has faith in you. It can take a while to get a grand-prize winner." She handed the pictures back to me.

I carefully returned them to the envelope. "Well, maybe there's a winner in my camera."

"Let's take a look."

I put the memory card in her computer and pulled up the new pictures. Some of the neighborhood, a few of Tasha, some of Kat, and the ones from that ill-fated trip to the Gorge. Well, ill-fated for Lissa, anyway. I set the folder to slide show, and leaned next to Gram to watch.

Gram shook her head at the pics of Tasha—"What an uncooperative cat!"—and laughed at the ones of Kat. "Ah, there's a good one." She pointed the image of Kat on a swing. "This shows her character, don't you think?"

"I ordered a print of that one."

When we got to the pictures from yesterday's outing, Gram oohed and aahed over the trees and waterfalls. When the ones of Lissa came up, Gram's hand flew to her mouth, and her eyes widened. "Oh my. Somebody does *not* look happy."

I giggled. "No, she wasn't a bit happy."

"And she will let you use those?" Gram looked over at me with questioning eyebrows.

"I didn't exactly show her and ask for permission."

Gram gave me one of those frowns that wasn't really a frown because her eyes were laughing. "Well, good luck with that, dear one."

I put the memory card back in my camera and helped Gram get up.

Face pale, she walked slowly over to the couch and sat down gingerly.

"Are you okay, Gram? You look tired."

"I *am* a bit tired. God gives me strength every day, though some days a little less than others." She winked. "But I don't need much. It's not like I have to go to work or anything."

Wait—wasn't I supposed to talk to her about going out? "Oh, Brett says hi. And he wanted me to invite you to his game tomorrow afternoon. Mom and Dad will be leaving for the beach, but Brett and I could take you. Can you come?"

She pursed her lips and narrowed her eyes a bit. "I don't know. I love to watch Brett play. He likes baseball the way you like taking photographs. Perhaps that's one of his God-given gifts. But I don't know if I will have the energy tomorrow."

"Please, Gram. You wouldn't have to do anything. Just sit there and watch."

She patted my hand. "Give me a call tomorrow, and I'll see how I feel—and what the weather looks like. Maybe I'll feel more energetic then."

I looked down and really saw our hands for the first time. Mine were smooth and tanned from being outside. Gram's were pale and wrinkled, with blue veins that snaked like raised rivers.

And yet her hands were beautiful in some strange

way because they reached out in love.

"Gram, can I take some pictures of you? You have a picture of me on your wall. I want to have a picture of you in my room at home. I especially want a picture of your hands."

Gram held her hands up and turned them to look at both sides. "Oh, these ugly old things? They've definitely seen better days."

"Well, I think they're beautiful." I took several pictures of Gram—her face, her hands, then all of her as she leaned on her cane by the window. I set the timer and took a couple of photos of both of us, racing over to get into the picture in time. Then I let her sit back down. "Can I take one more? One of both of our hands. One of mine and one of yours, I mean. I'll need my other hand to snap the shutter."

"Of course, dear one."

After I finished, I stuck the memory card back in the computer to check out the new pictures.

Gram watched in silence. A tear ran down her face.

"What's the matter? Are you all right?"

She put an arm around me. "Oh, yes, dear. I'm fine. Take these pictures in to Ray at the camera shop and see what he thinks."

"What do you think of them?"

She looked at me with shiny eyes. "I can't really judge because all I see is the love you put into them."

I gave Gram a big hug and didn't let go for a while. My pictures had never made anyone cry before. There was so much more to photography than I had realized when I first got that camera. The story behind the picture mattered as much as what was in it. And I knew

I wanted copies of the pictures of Gram, whether or not they were good enough for any contest.

I made a second stop at the camera shop on the way home.

When Mr. Browning put the memory card in his machine and looked at my new pictures, his face grew intent and serious. And then it creased in a smile. "Why, that's Rose, isn't it? You know Rose?"

"She's my great-grandma."

"Well, that explains your artistic streak. Rose used to come in here to get frames for her paintings. Such a wonderful lady. How is she?"

His words made me feel warm inside. Gram *was* a wonderful lady—he had that right. "She's doing fine, except that she was a bit tired today. She lives at Big Maples Retirement Home."

"How nice. I should stop by and see her someday. We used to have wonderful discussions about art and beauty." He got a far-off look on his face.

"She's the one who gave me my camera. She says I have a God-given gift for photography."

"Perhaps so." Mr. Browning looked back at the pictures on the screen. "You want to order some of these? I think you should."

I pointed to the ones I liked best, and he nodded and clicked on them. I asked how much they would cost. It would take most of my saved allowance to pay for the pictures and mats, but it would be worth it.

13

"Now remember, Aunt Lissa is in charge." Mom shivered a bit in the cool afternoon cloudiness and pulled on her jacket. Her eyes glowed with excitement, but she looked a bit nervous too.

Mom and Dad hadn't gone anywhere overnight in ages. They usually couldn't afford to. But somebody at Dad's factory had a beach house that he rented out cheap. This year Mom and Dad could finally get away for their anniversary. And Lissa being here meant they wouldn't have to leave us alone. Not that we couldn't have handled it—but Mom would have worried the whole time.

"Come on, Carol." Dad took Mom's arm. "Let's get going. Traffic is going to be heavy." Even Dad seemed excited, almost like Brett on his first date. Brett had pretended very hard *not* to be excited—just like Dad was now. Still, he gave it away by the way he pushed Mom toward the car.

Why had I left my camera inside? This would have made a great picture. *Happy Day* or something like that.

Mom turned back to hug me and Brett and Lissa.

Dad waved. "We'll be back Sunday afternoon."

"You guys be good. Keep the house clean and do your chores." Mom opened the car door. "Oh, and, Brett, have a good game tomorrow. Sorry we can't be there."

"No problem," Brett said. "JJ will cheer me on."

"Carol …" Dad slid into the driver's seat.

Brett and I waved as they pulled out of the driveway.

As we walked back into the kitchen, Brett grinned. "I got my paycheck from work today. Want to order a pizza?"

"Sure! Pepperoni, please."

From halfway down the hall, Lissa called out, "Order a large, and I'll pay for part of it."

Brett frowned and yelled back, "I can eat a large all by myself."

Lissa came back into the room. "Really?" Her eyebrows raised

I nodded. Lissa obviously did not know much about teenage boys.

"Okay. Order two larges, and I'll pay for one. Make sure you order mushrooms and artichokes on mine."

Artichokes? Yuck. Lissa and Brett could eat *that* pizza.

I hung out with Kat the next day while Brett worked. We cleaned her room together, which was quite a chore since Kat wasn't the world's neatest person. I pulled out a shirt—black, of course, but with a heart shape in pink sequins—from under her bed.

Kat's eyes lit up. "I've been looking for that."

"You might try cleaning your room more often." I threw the shirt at her.

Kat scrunched up her face. "Nah, not gonna happen."

I liked being in Kat's room, although it was very different from mine. She had a purple bedspread and dark blue walls covered with posters of rock stars. Most of the celebrities wore black and had spikes on their clothes. And some had rings and studs in various spots on their faces. I thought they looked kind of gross, but Kat said it showed they were rebels who thought for themselves and didn't become slaves to fashion. So I tried to think of the studs as good things. Kat wanted to get eyebrow studs, but her mom wouldn't let her.

It was another cloudy morning, but around eleven o'clock, little shafts of sunlight poked through the clouds. After a while, the holes widened into patches of blue. Maybe Gram would come to the game after all.

At noon, Kat and I headed over to my house. Mom had stocked up on good stuff like pop and chips to keep us happy while they were gone, so it seemed like the best place for lunch.

"I need to change clothes," I said. "I'm all dusty from crawling around on your floor and under your bed."

"Sorry." Looking anything but, she wrinkled her nose.

I headed down the hall, while she surveyed the cupboards. When I reached the room, I heard Lissa's voice inside and stopped. She must be talking on her cell phone. I put my ear close to the door. It wasn't exactly eavesdropping, was it? After all, it was *my* room.

"I can't move back. You know what happened at work. I could never get a job down there." She was silent a moment, probably listening to the other person. "No, I don't want the law getting involved."

86

Kat started down the hall. "Hey, I thought you were gonna change."

Frantically, I waved her back, finger to my lips.

She stopped short, looking confused.

From inside the room I heard, "Got to go. I think somebody's home."

Yikes! I couldn't let her find me outside the door. I tiptoed out of there at top speed, probably looking really silly, until I reached the kitchen.

"What on Earth, Mars, and the moon is going on?" Kat asked, hands on hips.

I glanced back but Lissa hadn't come out yet. "I heard Lissa on the phone," I whispered. "She said she couldn't get a job back in California and that she didn't want the law involved."

Kat's eyes almost exploded, they got so big. "She *did* break the law. That's why she got fired."

"It sure sounds suspicious. What are we going to do?" I kept looking back at my room. Lissa might walk out at any moment and figure out that I had heard.

"We could call the police."

"But we don't even know what she did."

"Oh yeah. I guess that wouldn't work." Kat tilted her head, eyes narrowed. "I think we need to investigate more. Criminals don't deserve privacy."

"I guess." Snooping still didn't seem right.

Lissa might be lazy, but she didn't seem like a criminal. On the other hand, why would she want to keep the law out of it?

If only Mom were home to talk to. She'd know what to do. Wait, what about Gram? She was the wisest person I knew. "I can ask Gram about it. She'll know what's right."

After lunch I took our old cordless phone and went out to the backyard, close enough for the phone to work, but far enough away that Lissa wouldn't hear if she had the window open.

Kat followed me out and watched the house while I made the call.

When Gram answered, she still sounded tired.

"Are you okay, Gram? I called to see if you wanted to go to Brett's game."

"I'm afraid I'm still pretty worn out. I'm so sorry. It looks like a perfect day for a game. Maybe next week."

I slumped down and kicked at the ground. Rats. It was such fun to watch Gram cheer at a game. Even Mom and Dad didn't get that excited.

But it was no use pleading. When Gram decided something, she rarely changed her mind.

"I have another question," I said quietly, looking toward Kat, who nodded that I could go ahead. "What do you do if you think somebody broke the law, but you're not sure?"

There was silence for a moment. "Somebody you know or somebody you saw on the street?"

"Somebody I know. Somebody who got fired from a job, maybe for doing something illegal." I wondered how much I should say.

"You mean Lissa, don't you?"

"Yes." Gram always figured out what I really meant.

"How do you know she got fired?"

And she would figure out if I lied too. "Kat and I were snooping. I know we shouldn't have, but we were curious and bored. We saw an email that said she was

88

fired. And I heard her talking on the phone about not wanting the law involved. Now I don't know what to do."

"My dear girl, they say a little knowledge is a dangerous thing, and I believe this may be a good example."

"What do you mean?"

"I mean you only know a tiny part of the story, don't you? And now you're turning that into a picture that may not be at all accurate."

"But you don't get fired for doing something good."

Gram was quiet so long I started to think I'd lost the connection. She spoke very softly. "Sweetie, I know you mean well. But remember, Lissa is my granddaughter. I believe in her as much as I believe in you. She makes mistakes, like we all do, but she's not a bad person. Give her a chance."

"So do nothing?"

"You might try praying about it."

"I don't know much about praying. Could you pray for me?"

"I will do that, JJ, gladly. Now I need to go rest. Be wise, dear one."

"I'll try, Gram," I said, and I really did mean it.

Kat seemed disappointed when I told her what Gram had said. Probably because Kat wanted to snoop some more. She watched a lot of detective shows on TV and thought there was a bad guy behind every bush.

But what *had* Lissa done to get fired?

And how could I find out without getting in trouble?

According to my watch, Brett would be home

anytime.

"Let's go pack some snacks for the game."

"Beat you to the kitchen!" Kat hollered and took off.

14

While Brett warmed up with the team, Kat and I threw an old blanket on the bleachers and started munching on pretzels. I got my camera ready, erasing some of the old pictures I didn't like.

Kat guarded our place while I got some pre-game photos.

I snapped some of Brett fielding grounders, and more of batting practice, but I couldn't get close enough to get any detail. Someday I would have a camera with a telephoto lens, and then I could get great pictures of all sorts of faraway things.

As Brett's team clattered off the field to let the visiting team warm up, I wandered over toward him. I didn't want to bug Brett—or the coach—so I hung back.

Brett motioned me over and faced his team. "Hey, guys!"

A couple of players looked his way.

"This is JJ. She's my paparazzi section today, so feel free to pose for pictures when she's not busy taking mine."

A couple of the guys who knew me grinned. One of them struck a pose like he was ready to catch a ball.

I snapped his picture.

Brett grabbed a bat and posed out on the grass.

If I got low, maybe I could capture the feeling of

power as he swung the bat. The angle made Brett a silhouette against the sky, and he looked larger than life.

He went along with it for a few photos, then let me know with a sigh and a frown that he was done. Warm-ups ended, and Brett grabbed his mitt and headed for second base, his usual position.

I meandered back to Kat and plopped onto the bench.

For most of the game, I sat with Kat and cheered for the team. Brett hit a triple one time and knocked in two runs, which made us scream our heads off. Whenever Brett came up to bat, I got behind the backstop and tried to get a photo through the chain-link fence.

His first couple of times up, Brett tipped his hat to me as he was getting set in the batter's box. About midway through the game, however, he motioned with his head toward the bleachers.

I got the hint.

When I settled back onto the bench, Kat turned to me. "I still think we need to find out more about you-know-who."

"But how?" We couldn't go through her stuff—not after talking to Gram. Besides, Lissa would be furious if she found out. And so would Mom.

"I could call and pretend to be a job place wanting her to apply."

"Right. A 'job place.' Now that sounds official. Yeah, she'd believe that."

Kat punched me in the arm. "Okay, bad idea. Since you don't want to snoop, how 'bout if I do the snooping and you keep watch?"

I shook my head. "I'd still be an accessory to the crime." Hmm. Maybe I'd been watching too many detective shows myself.

"Well, you could interrogate her. With a bright light overhead and all that. Like in the police shows."

"I'm not a police officer, and I don't think Lissa would agree to an interrogation."

Kat looked disappointed. "Too bad. I was going to suggest the 'good cop, bad cop' method. I'd play the bad cop, of course."

"You'd make a good bad cop. Wait, that doesn't sound right. 'You'd be good at being a bad cop'?"

"Yeah, that's it. It's my inborn acting talent. Great actors always like to try out the role of a bad guy."

Another idea came to me. "I can't interrogate Lissa, but I could talk to her more, you know, like I want to get to know her. I might find out something that way."

"Snooping would be more efficient, though." She cocked her head and gave me a hopeful, eyebrows-raised look.

I shook my head.

Her face fell. "Oh well. Whatever."

Brett's team was ahead and the game was almost over, so I walked toward the dugout for some end-of-game shots. Too bad it wasn't a championship game. It would have been great to get a pic of all the players jumping up, screaming, and falling over each other. That wasn't likely to happen for an ordinary mid-season game. The home team center fielder caught the ball, ending the inning and the game. *Home 6, Visitors 3.*

I took pictures as the guys trotted in, giving each other high-fives. The sun setting in the background added a nice touch. Maybe I would have one or two pictures worthy of entering. As for a grand-prize winner—probably not in this bunch.

We stopped for burgers on our way home. Brett bought again, since he was the only one with money, but he made me promise to do his laundry to repay him. He was supposed to be saving his money for college, but he didn't always get around to putting it in his savings account. He said he figured he'd get a baseball scholarship anyway.

When we got home, Kat said good-bye. Brett headed for the shower, and I started cleaning up the family room, my extra weekend chore. I thought about going back to my room and talking to Lissa, but decided to get my job done first. Mom might be grumpy if she returned to a messy family room.

I had just finished dusting when Lissa barged in, face beaming like the sun. "My boyfriend's coming to visit. He'll be here next Saturday."

"Here? He's not staying *here*, is he?" Where would he sleep? In Brett's room? Good luck finding enough space to stretch out in there.

"Oh, no." She laughed. "He'll stay at a motel. Don't worry. You'll like him, I'm sure. Everyone likes Thomas. I'll have to take him to see Multnomah Falls … or maybe Mount Hood. If I can get him to fall in love with Oregon, maybe he'll move up here." She spun around like a dancer, then pranced back to the bedroom.

Why did girls get so goofy over guys, even grown-up ladies like Lissa? Mom said it would happen to me anytime now. No way. Oh, it would be fine to like boys and go on dates. But I did *not* want to get all dreamy-eyed and stupid-headed. Surely a girl could be in love and still be sane.

Then I remembered my secret assignment: get to know Lissa. This would be the perfect time. She was happy, so her guard would be down. Maybe she would slip up and say something that would give me a clue about what happened down in California.

I put the dust cloth away and walked back to the bedroom.

Lissa sat at her computer, as usual, but she wasn't typing, just staring at it with kind of a silly smile on her face.

"What's your boyfriend like?" I sat down on my bed.

That must have been a good first question because her eyes lit up more, and she gave a quiet, little sigh. "He's great. Kind and caring. Good at his job. And he loves kids."

"What's it like having a boyfriend? Do you do a lot of things together?"

"Of course." She leaned back a bit in her chair and smoothed her golden hair. "We like to go to the movies, out to dinner, hiking ... all sorts of things."

Maybe it would be safe to probe a little deeper. "Do you tell him all your secrets?"

Lissa's eyes narrowed the slightest bit.

Oops. Couldn't let her catch on to what I was doing. "I mean, you're supposed to share things, right? I've never had a boyfriend, so I don't know much about it."

She laughed.

Good. She thought I was actually curious about boyfriends and all that. She was easier to trick than

Mom—maybe because she didn't have kids yet.

"Yes, we share lots of things. I tell him when I have a bad day at work. He tells me when he gets mad at a driver on the freeway. And we talk about what we want to do in the future."

"So he's a good listener?"

"Oh, definitely. That's an important quality to find in a boyfriend."

"Good to know." Yes, very good. If I couldn't find out the truth from Lissa, maybe I could get it from her boyfriend. Maybe he would be as good a talker as he was a listener. "Where did you meet him? At work?"

"No." Her face clouded over for a moment. Like she didn't want to even think about work. No surprise there. "No, I met him through a friend. He works for the newspaper."

Probably best to stop while I was ahead—at least for now. "Nice. Well, I guess I'll meet him next week." I stood up and stretched. "I'm going to go check on Tasha."

Tasha was curled up on the couch in the family room.

I sat down and patted her head, then scratched her under the chin.

Tasha purred and leaned into my hand.

Soon Brett walked in, smelling like soap and aftershave, and sat on the other side of the cat.

She slashed her tail but kept purring. Brett wasn't her favorite person, probably because he never sat still for long. His lap was not a dependable place to settle.

"Good game, huh?" A satisfied grin covered his face.

"The best." I kept on petting Tasha.

96

Brett turned on the TV and channel surfed until he found a show with lots of action and a car chase.

I gave Tasha a final pat and wandered outside. Sitting on the steps, I stared up at the starry sky. Were Mom and Dad walking on the beach under the stars right now? I missed hearing their voices in the kitchen, feeling a pat on the back from Mom as she walked past, and even smelling Dad's coffee in the morning.

Family are the people you belong to, whether you like it or not. But mostly you do.

Gram said something like that often, and it felt right. Mom might get grumpy sometimes, and Dad might ignore me too often, but I belonged to them and they belonged to me, and it would be nice to have them back home.

The temperature had dropped quickly. Shivering, I stayed on the porch a few minutes longer. I was so tired I had to keep blinking to keep my eyes open.

Time to go to bed. Maybe tomorrow I could work on Lissa's secrets some more.

15

As I woke up Sunday morning and the fuzziness cleared from my mind, I remembered my dream. It had been a beautiful day, the sunshine glittering like gold on the edges of the tree trunks, the sky a bright summer blue. Gram and I were walking to church, just like we used to when I was little and had spent the night at her house. In my dream I was in her church again, feeling as if angels were all around me.

Her church really did have stained-glass windows, and the morning sun would light them up. If the sermons got boring—they weren't aimed at five-year-olds, after all—I would get lost in those windows, trying to catch a glimpse of heaven through them.

Still lying in bed, I closed my eyes and tried to return to the dream, but it was too late. I opened my eyes and sighed, all warm and tingly inside.

Was that bacon cooking? I sat up. Were Mom and Dad home already?

But they had said they'd be back in the afternoon.

I pulled back the curtain and looked over at Lissa's bed. Was she up there? I climbed the ladder to look, but her bed was empty. Could Lissa actually be fixing breakfast?

I got dressed and headed down the hall. It *was* Lissa! And judging by the amount of bacon in the pan, she was cooking for all of us.

"Hey, kid. Hungry?"

For once I didn't mind being called "kid" because that bacon smelled really good.

Lissa was beating some eggs. A bowl of grated cheese waited at the side and bread sat in the toaster.

"Yes, I *am* hungry. Really hungry."

"Good. Why don't you wake up that lazybones brother of yours and see if he wants to eat with us." She winked.

I grinned, skipped down the hall, and banged on Brett's door.

"Go away," a muffled voice called.

"Wake up if you want breakfast. Lissa's making bacon and eggs." The one thing Brett liked as well as sleep was food. There was probably a real battle going on in his head—sleep or food?

"Bacon and eggs?" The voice was a little less muffled, like he had at least pulled the covers off his head.

"That's what I said."

A movement, then a big thump that sounded like someone falling out of bed.

I giggled. Brett was pretty funny when he was trying to wake up. "Are you okay?"

"Uh, yeah, I think so. I'll be right out. Don't eat without me."

"You'd better hurry, then." I laughed and ran back to the kitchen. I helped set the table while Lissa cut up an orange and scrambled the eggs.

True to his word, Brett was soon out, wearing his usual shorts, T-shirt, and rumpled hair.

I ate slowly, savoring the crunchy, salty bacon and

chewy, cheesy eggs. Mom rarely had time to fix a hot breakfast, and she said bacon wasn't good for us anyway, so this was a real treat. I grabbed an extra bacon strip before Brett could empty the plate. He ate enough for a family of four, so I had to be quick.

Lissa seemed really cheerful this morning. Apparently boyfriend visits did that to ladies.

Well, if it made her cook more, I was all for it.

Tasha jumped up on my lap, begging for food.

I slipped her a little piece of bacon and a chunk of egg when Lissa wasn't looking. Cats deserved treats too. After breakfast I cleaned up the kitchen, which was rather messy. Lissa still wasn't into cleaning up, but she *did* make breakfast, so I wasn't too annoyed.

Brett stuck a few things in the dishwasher, which was a lot of help considering he didn't have to do all the chores I did. Work and sports and all.

My dream came back into my head. It had seemed so real. Kat might like to hear about it, but Sunday was mother-daughter day at her house, so I couldn't call her. She and her mom always spent the day either going someplace or doing things together at home. If only I could have a mother-daughter day ...

Maybe when Mom got her teaching certificate.

I ambled down the hall to my room. But those stained-glass windows were stuck in my head. I wanted to see them again.

Well, why not?

I pulled the curtain across the room and changed into a nice pair of pants and a white blouse.

When I opened the curtain again, Lissa glanced over, then twisted all the way around. "You look dressed up."

100

"I'm going to go see Gram, and I thought I would dress up a bit since it's Sunday. They have a church service at her place, and it might still be going on when I get there."

"Oh, okay. But don't be too long. Your parents should be back by three or four."

I nodded and headed out to my bike. The sun was warm on my face, and the sky was clear blue. The fresh breeze carried a hint of rose blossom scent from the bush by the corner of the house. When I came to the road to Gram's retirement home, I stopped for a moment, but I didn't turn that way. Instead, I kept riding for another quarter mile or so and then turned onto a busy street with a bike lane. I ended up in front of a small brick building with a steeple rising up in front and a cross on top.

Gram's old church.

It still looked the same, exactly how it had looked in my dream. For a second I was five years old again, and life was wonderful. I pushed my bike around the building, chained it to a railing in back, and returned to the front. After checking to make sure my pants and blouse were still clean, I carefully eased open the door and slipped into the foyer.

The doors to the sanctuary were open, and the pastor's voice carried into the lobby.

I crept closer until I could see the stained-glass windows. They were as beautiful as ever. I slid quietly into the back pew.

A couple of old ladies looked over, and one of them smiled at me.

I smiled back.

The pastor kept talking, but his voice faded to a dull hum against my thoughts. I drank in the bright colors as the sun streamed through the windows that seemed to be connected to heaven.

When the service ended, the pastor walked to the back of the church before I could slip out the door. "Good morning." He reached out and shook my hand. "I'm so glad you came to visit. What brought you here today?" He was about my dad's age with dark eyes and warm hands.

"My great-grandma used to come to this church. I wanted to see if it was still here." That sounded stupid. Why had I come anyway? Could a person be homesick for a place that wasn't home? That's kind of what it felt like.

"Who is your great-grandma?"

"Rose Warren."

His smile got bigger. "Sweet Rose. Such a wonderful lady. It's been years since I've heard her name. Is she … I mean, does she still live around here?"

What he really meant was, is she still alive? But there was no polite way to ask that. I nodded. "She's at Big Maples Retirement Home. She goes to church there now."

The pastor seemed to relax. "Well, please tell her that Pastor Bob sends his best." He shook my hand again.

"I will." As quickly as possible, I was back on my bike, speeding toward Gram's.

When I entered the retirement home, there was a different receptionist than usual. "Who have you come to visit?"

"My great-grandma, Rose Warren."

She looked down at a list. "This might not be a good day. Mrs. Warren isn't feeling well. We've asked the nurse to check in on her."

My heart thumped a couple of extra beats. "It's okay. I won't stay long. And I'll be really quiet."

"I guess that would be fine, then."

When I got up to Gram's room, I rang the bell but didn't hear an answer. Maybe she was sleeping. Should I go home? But I decided to try one more time.

This time, I heard a faint "Please come in."

The door was unlocked.

I walked in.

Gram wasn't in the living room, so I checked the bedroom. She was lying in bed. When she saw me, she pushed a pillow behind her back and sat up a bit. "Why, JJ, I didn't expect you today." She looked pale and tired, even more than the other day.

I pulled a chair up to the bed and sat down.

She reached toward me.

I took her cold hand and pressed it between my warm ones. "Are you okay, Gram?" I hadn't seen her that low on energy since she had the flu last year. Gram was always so full of life. "Are you sick?"

"Well, dear, I think I may be. The nurse is coming to check on me. Perhaps I've caught a cold or something." Even her smile looked exhausted.

"I dreamed about you last night."

A little spark came back to her eyes. "Really? I hope it was a good dream."

"Of course it was. I dreamed I was little, it was a beautiful day, and we were walking to your church like we used to."

"How nice."

"I stopped at that church this morning. I got there for the last part of the service. The stained-glass windows are just as pretty as I remembered. And Pastor Bob says hi."

A pale glow lit Gram's face. "Oh, I'm so glad you were in church. Nice to know Pastor Bob is still there." She paused to take a breath. "You know, sometimes God sends dreams. Maybe He is calling you back."

"Really? God would do that? Send a dream 'specially to me?" I got goose bumps, in spite of the warm day. Could my dream have been a message from God?

"He might. And He might have sent it for me too." She looked out the window at the sky. "Maybe He's calling me."

"What do you mean, Gram? He doesn't need to call you back. You're always close to Him."

She squeezed my hand. "Dear one, remember that dream. It can be a comfort to you when you feel lonely. Remember, God believes in you."

I nodded, but a lump stuck in my throat. What did Gram mean, that I might feel lonely? She couldn't be *that* sick. I squeezed her hand back.

The doorbell rang.

I let go of Gram's hand and answered the door.

It was the nurse.

Gram slid back down to a lying position. "I think you should go, JJ. The nurse will check me over. Then I think I'll take a nap."

I nodded and started to leave but ran back and hugged Gram. "I love you."

"And I love you too, dear one."

I hurried to leave before she could see the tears in my eyes. "I'll come back tomorrow," I called as I left. I couldn't hear if she answered.

16

When I got home from Gram's, I changed into shorts and a T-shirt, found Tasha, and carried her over to the couch. I settled her on my lap and stroked her soft, black-and-white fur, taking deep breaths.

Gram would be better soon. Last year she was really sick with the flu for two or three days, but it didn't last. This wouldn't either. It couldn't.

The second hand on the wall clock crept along. I kept petting Tasha until she meowed at me, jumped off my lap, and stalked away down the hall.

Why did that stupid clock move so slowly? When would Mom and Dad get home? Mom would tell me not to be silly, that Gram would be fine. Mom's voice always made things seem more real than the voice in my own head.

Finally, the familiar chugging of our old car sounded in the driveway.

I ran to the back door and stepped outside, closing the door behind me. When Mom got out of the car, I practically jumped on her, giving her a big hug.

She looked at me with wide eyes. "Well, it's nice to be welcomed home so enthusiastically. Did you miss me?"

"A little." I stepped back. Didn't want her to think I was a little kid who couldn't be away from her mommy. Twelve-year-olds should be more mature than that.

"Was the beach fun?"

Mom looked at Dad.

They both looked like kids who'd come out of a candy store with a full bag of treats.

"Oh, yes. We had nice weather, and it was great to get down there," she said. Her face looked younger without the usual worry lines. It *must* have been a good weekend.

Dad patted me on the head, then pulled their suitcases out of the back seat.

Mom handed me a small, white paper bag. "We bought you guys some saltwater taffy. I got plenty of the chocolate-peanut butter kind you like."

I peeked inside. "Thanks. I better hide some of these from Brett, or he'll gobble them down before I have a chance to have any." I closed the bag quickly and hugged it to my chest.

After they unpacked, Mom and Dad listened to the rest of us tell about our weekend. Brett described his game, and Lissa jabbered on about Thomas coming to visit. I told about visiting Gram and how the nurse had come to see her.

The worry lines returned to Mom's forehead. "Maybe I'll run over and check on her."

"I'll come with you," I said.

Mom shook her head. "If she's not feeling well, one person at a time is enough. I'll let you know how she's doing."

But when Mom got home from visiting Gram, she didn't have much to say. Just that Gram was tired and that the nurse said she needed to stay in bed and rest. If that was all the nurse had said, why was Mom frowning? Did I really want to ask? When Mom caught me staring at her, she smiled and rubbed my back like she used to do when I was little and sick in bed.

It didn't help.

Mom picked a DVD for the whole family to watch, and we laughed our way through the funny movie. Dad made popcorn and I snuggled up close to Mom. Brett squinted at me, like he was going to tease me but kept quiet. Even Lissa joined us, and, for once, I didn't mind.

The next morning Mom's engine started up extra early, waking me. I glanced at the clock and frowned. Why would she be leaving now? I fell back to sleep before I could do too much thinking. When I finally got up, the morning was well underway.

Lissa went off to another job interview.

Please hire her, people!

She'd also applied for several jobs online but had no luck there yet.

Brett wasn't up, but music seeped from under his bedroom door as if he was trying to wake up.

How was Gram today?

The nurse had said Gram needed rest. Maybe after lunch would be the best time to visit.

I ate a bowl of cereal and then went next door to see if Kat was up.

Amazingly enough, she was not only up, but also dressed. Today, instead of her usual black, she wore a purple T-shirt with a multi-colored, sequin butterfly on the front.

"Nice shirt. It's almost cheerful."

"I felt like a change today. Purple is still dark, so it works. Although I guess the butterfly is a little out of character."

"Yeah, you have such a dark personality."

Kat rolled her eyes and stuck out her tongue. "Yep, I'm a pretty depressing person. Pretty scary too." She let loose a *bwa-ha-ha* laugh from deep in her throat.

I chuckled. Kat was always good at cheering me up.

We wandered back to my house and spent the rest of the morning at the computer, looking at my recent photographs. Kat loved the ones of Lissa falling into the creek, but I made her promise not to breathe a word to Lissa. Too risky. We chose our two favorite baseball pictures—one of Brett swinging his bat, and one of him and a teammate giving high-fives after the game. Brett's expressions were so different, total concentration in the first and a burst of joy in the second. *Victory* would be a good title for that one.

I had taken a few more pics of Tasha, and Kat and I chose two of those. If I took them to the camera shop on my way to Gram's that afternoon, they should be ready in time for the contest. I could enter them on Friday and hold my breath until Saturday when the winners would be announced.

Oh, God, please let me win. I really want that new camera.

When I clicked out of the photo program, Kat turned to me with an expectant look. "So, how's the snooping—er, getting to know Lissa—going? Any new info?"

"Not really. She doesn't want to talk about her old job. But her boyfriend is coming to visit on Saturday."

"Ooh." Kat rubbed her hands together. "Maybe he'll talk, even if she won't. We'll get to the bottom of this."

I pretended to adjust a monocle. "I do say, old chap, we shall indeed."

Kat laughed at my impression of Sherlock Holmes, then wiggled her fingers, reaching for my armpit while my hand was still up to my face.

I tickled her back, and soon we were rolling around on the floor like a couple of little kids and laughing like hyenas.

All our racket finally got Brett up to see what was going on. He shook his head and started to turn away but I called him over.

I showed him the baseball pictures, but *not* the waterfall—or should I say *Lissa-fall*—ones.

Lissa walked in the back door as we were finishing lunch. This time she was smiling.

"How'd the interview go?" I crossed my fingers.

"Pretty well. They want me back for a second interview on Thursday. That's always a good sign."

I gave her a high-five and grinned over at Kat. Yes, oh yes!

Brett winked at me. He'd probably be glad to see her gone too.

"After lunch, I'm riding over to see Gram," I told Lissa.

She looked at me. "Why don't you wait until I get something to eat? I was going to go see her, and I could drive you over."

"But I need to stop at the camera shop."

"That's fine. I can wait while you do your business

110

there."

"I'd like to come too." Brett looked over at Lissa. "I haven't been by to see her for a while."

"Sure. No problem."

My stomach tightened. Brett rarely visited Gram. Lissa had only been over once for a quick visit since coming to Oregon. Why the sudden interest? "Did Mom tell you something she didn't tell me? Is Gram really, really sick?"

"I want to go cheer her up, that's all." Lissa headed for our room before I could ask anything more.

I looked at Kat, who stared back at me.

Neither of us said a word. This could not be good.

17

"We're here to see Rose Warren," Lissa told the usual receptionist at the retirement home. "We're family."

Brett nodded, fidgeting like the place made him nervous.

"I know," the lady said, nodding at me. She might not recognize Lissa or Brett, but she definitely knew me. "Yes, you may go up. The nurse was by and left the door unlocked, so just go on in. Rose is probably resting."

I led the way to her room, wishing Kat had come too.

Gram was lying in bed with two pillows propping her head up a bit. Her eyes were closed, and her face looked really old—kind of gray and more wrinkled than I had ever noticed. Her uncombed hair stuck out in places like Brett's hair first thing in the morning.

My throat tightened, making it hard to swallow.

Gram opened her eyes and gave us a soft smile. "Well, I feel popular today. Three visitors at once."

"We were worried about you, Gram." I settled into a chair by the bed while Lissa and Brett stayed standing. I reached out and took Gram's hand. It was way too cold.

She squeezed weakly. "Well, you know what they say," she said with a little chuckle. "I'll either get better or I'll die."

"Gram! Don't say that." I blinked back the tears that formed.

"Dear one, it's all right. I've already lived longer than most people. I've had loving family and a rewarding life." She squeezed my hand again. "And I know where I'm going when I die. So it's nothing to be sad about."

"But you *can* get better."

"I might. Or I might not. Either way, it's in the Lord's hands, and I trust Him."

"And He believes in you, doesn't He, Gram?"

"Yes, He does, sweetie." She looked over at Brett and Lissa. "Brett, dear, how was your game? I'm so sorry I missed it."

"Great." His voice sounded deep and scratchy. "We clobbered them, and I hit a triple."

"That's my boy." Gram looked at Lissa. "And how is the job search coming?"

"I had a good interview this morning, Grandma." Lissa reached over and took Gram's other hand. "They want me to come back for a second one."

"I know you'll get a nice job. You're a smart girl. And a good one. Don't forget that."

Lissa nodded silently and cleared her throat.

"Well, dears," Gram said after a moment. "I'm sorry to send you away so soon, but I think I need to rest. I'm feeling so tired today. Thank you all for coming."

I stood up, so Lissa could lean over and hug Gram.

Lissa left the room, and Brett gave Gram a hug—something I hadn't seen him do since he was twelve. "Love you, Gram," he whispered. He joined Lissa in the living room, leaving me alone with Gram.

I bent over, wrapped my arms around her, and listened to her heartbeat. Why did I have to leave so soon? I hurt inside like I was watching a really sad movie—but this was real life.

That made it a lot worse.

"I love you so much, Gram," I whispered.

"I know you do, sweet Jada Jane. Did you know that your middle name means 'God is gracious'?"

I sat up on the bed and looked at her. "Nobody ever told me that."

"Remember it, dear one, because it's true. And remember that I love you dearly. And God loves you even more."

"And He believes in me?" I forced a wobbly smile.

"We both do. Go enjoy your day. I'll be fine."

I hugged her one more time and walked out slowly, stopping to wave from the doorway.

On the way home, we stopped at Ray's Camera Shop. Lissa and Brett waited in the car while I went in.

A man was asking about cameras, so I had to wait. Finally, the man decided he would look around some more before buying and left.

Mr. Browning motioned me over. "JJ, right?"

I nodded.

"Your prints won't be ready until tomorrow."

"I know. I have a couple more to order. Well, three actually. Two for the sports category and one for animals." I handed him the memory card from my camera and told him which numbers I wanted.

He brought the images up. "These should be good contenders."

"For the grand prize?" I held my breath. Could it

really be true?

"Well, I don't know about that. But in the kids' category, they could win something."

My breath came out in a long sigh. "I really, really want to win the grand prize. I need that camera." I ached inside at the thought. Or maybe I really ached for Gram—but that reason was too painful to give a thought to. Either way, I'd been aching too much lately.

"Well, who knows? It's all up to the judges. But I can have these ready for you Thursday afternoon."

"Thanks. I'll need some more mats for them." I glanced around the store. "But I don't have time to look."

Lissa was probably drumming her fingers on the steering wheel, wondering what was taking so long. And Brett would be staring out the window, frowning. A picture titled *Impatience*.

"Don't worry. I'll pick out some good mats for you."

"Thanks." I took back the memory card, put it in the camera, and ran out to the car.

And, yes, my mental picture of the car scene had been accurate.

When we got home, I stuck the camera in my pocket, trotted over to the school, and threw myself into a swing. When I was upset or nervous about something, sometimes I would swing higher and higher until the whole world disappeared, and the only things left were me and the sky.

I started pumping my legs, back and forth, back and forth. The breeze cooled my face. My hair flew out behind me as I glided forward and swept against my cheeks when I went back. I closed my eyes and enjoyed the rocking motion of the swing.

Back and forth, back and forth I went, losing myself in the clouds, escaping the earth below. And up there in the sky, I felt certain that Gram would be fine, that she would be there to cheer me on for a long time.

God, please make her better—really, really soon. I need her.

Something hit me in the back like a dozen tiny insect bites all at once.

I dropped out of the clouds and opened my eyes, looking around as the swing jerked out of rhythm.

Kat stood there, grinning and holding a handful of bark dust, apparently ready to give me another shower if I didn't acknowledge her.

"Hi, Kat." I slowed to a stop. I felt as if I'd woken from a dream and wasn't quite sure where I was.

"Wanna go to the store and get some ice cream?"

"I don't have any money."

Kat waved a five-dollar bill in the air before sticking it back in her pants' pocket. "I got my allowance. My treat."

The sun had grown warm, and I felt a bit sweaty from all that swinging, so I swallowed my fears and walked down the street toward the little neighborhood store at the end of the block.

"How's Gram?"

"She's pretty sick. But I think she's going to be all right." The more I thought about it, the truer it felt. I could picture her, bent over a jigsaw puzzle, the sunlight touching her hair like a halo.

She *had* to be all right, and so she would. She could wait to die until I was all grown-up. It would be easier for me then.

116

"Any more inside info on that aunt of yours?" Kat looked around as if to make sure no one was listening.

I shook my head. "I'm afraid she seems pretty normal. A bit annoying at times, but not like a criminal."

"That's what they *want* you to think," Kat hissed in a low voice.

"They?"

"Criminals. You know how, when somebody gets arrested for a crime, they always interview the neighbors on TV? And the neighbors always say, 'He seemed like such a nice guy'? You can't go by that. She could be a bank robber, for all we know." Her eyes narrowed, and she pressed her lips together.

I stared at Kat. "I think you're getting a little carried away. Maybe she goofed off too much or something, but I'm sure she never robbed any bank."

"Don't be too sure." Kat looked around again. "It's the quiet ones you can't trust."

"She's actually not that quiet."

We reached the little store and turned our attention to choosing ice cream. Kat picked out a Creamsicle, and I chose a chocolate-covered ice cream bar. We ate them slowly as we walked home. Then we settled onto the bench by the picnic table in my backyard.

I was about to say something when a voice drifted from the house. It sounded like Lissa's.

I put a finger to my lips, crept toward the house, and sneaked along the outside toward my bedroom.

Kat followed.

My bedroom window was open.

As we got closer, Lissa's voice grew louder. She didn't sound happy. "They can't do that. It's not right."

A pause.

Okay, she was on the phone.

"I know I shouldn't have done it, but I did. It's too late to change it."

Kat's eyebrows shot up.

"As long as I keep quiet, nobody ever has to know. I just want to forget it and start fresh up here."

Kat leaned forward, pressing against me. She didn't need to take up all the space.

I nudged her back, maybe a little hard.

Then she pushed me.

I lost my balance and crashed forward into the bushes. As I picked myself up, Lissa yelled out the window, "What's going on out there?"

"We were playing." I brushed off my shirt. "Kat was chasing me, and I fell down." It was only half a lie. It *was* Kat's fault I fell down.

"Come in here, JJ," Lissa shouted. "I need to talk to you."

I stood up and looked at Kat.

"Well, gotta go," she said. "Uh, I'll see you later." She backed a few steps away from the house and added in a whisper, "Good luck!"

I frowned at Kat as she turned to leave. Some friend, deserting me when I got in hot water.

But it might be for the best. At least we wouldn't need to coordinate alibis. I walked very slowly into the house, planning out what to say. If I could get Lissa to believe we were running around, she might believe we didn't hear anything. It *could* work.

I pulled my camera out of my pocket on the way down the hall, checking to make sure it hadn't been damaged by the fall.

It still worked.

Whew! I walked into the bedroom and set the camera on my nightstand. "What do you want?" I asked, making my voice as innocent-sounding as possible.

"Were you guys listening in on me out there?" Lissa stared at me, eyes narrowed.

"We were just playing around. Why? Were you talking to somebody?"

"What makes you think that?" she asked, taking a step closer.

Oops. Bad choice of words on my part. "Nothing. I figured if you thought we were listening, that you must have been talking."

"I suppose that makes sense." She didn't look convinced. "Look, I just want my privacy."

"Well, so do I. But I got stuck sharing my room with you." It sounded mean, but so what? Visiting Gram had made me feel like a balloon that had been pumped too full of air and was ready to burst at the slightest touch. Every annoying thing Lissa had done piled up on top of that balloon, stretching it to the limit.

Lissa put her hands on her hips and glared at me. "Well, you're not always the best roommate yourself. In fact, you can be a bit of a brat sometimes."

That did it. The balloon burst, and all the anger and hurt and fear came spewing out. I grabbed my pillow, swung it back, and threw it at Lissa with all my strength.

Unfortunately—or fortunately for Lissa—a pillow was not a very good weapon.

She jumped out of the way, leaned down, and

picked it up. "I'll be out of here as soon as I can," she said in what was barely under a yell. "But until then, you'd better learn to put up with it." And she threw my pillow back at me.

I raised my hand and deflected it.

It flopped onto my nightstand and onto the floor with a very unpillowlike clunk.

Panic shot through me.

A pillow doesn't clunk, but ...

My camera no longer sat on the nightstand.

18

I dropped to my knees, grabbed the pillow, and tossed it to the side.

There lay my camera on the floor.

It couldn't be broken! Heart pounding, I took a deep breath and picked it up.

It had landed with the lens facing up, and that side appeared fine.

I let my breath out. Maybe the camera would be okay. I turned it over.

Jagged cracks covered the screen, and one corner was smashed in.

I pressed the power button.

Nothing happened.

My insides seemed to bend and crack like the camera. What was I going to do? How could I record my life, capture moments of beauty, make the pictures that were more true than reality? Gram had given me that camera, and now it was useless.

I turned on Lissa. "You broke my camera!" Anger boiled up and spilled out as I glared at her.

Lissa stared back at me, mouth open. "I ... I didn't mean to. You ... you threw the pillow first. I ..." Tears filled her eyes. "I'm sorry."

She started toward me, but I waved her off. "Get away from me. Just get away." I yanked the curtain across the room to separate us.

"JJ, I didn't mean to. Maybe it can be fixed. I'll pay to have it fixed."

I lay on my bed, holding my camera, and sobbed. "Life isn't fair."

"JJ," Lissa pleaded from behind the curtain. "Please let me come in."

"Go away!" I yelled. "Just go away." I couldn't stand to look at her.

It was silent for a minute before Lissa's footsteps left the room and faded down the hall.

The tears kept coming—for the camera, for Gram, for losing my privacy, and for everything all smashed together. The room closed in around me as I curled up into a ball on the bed.

Later, after I was too tired to cry anymore, footsteps entered the room. "JJ?" This time it was Mom's voice.

I pushed myself up to a sitting position and wiped my eyes. "Yeah?"

Mom pushed aside the curtain and sat on my bed. She put her arm around me, and I leaned into her. "Lissa said your camera got broken. She feels really bad about it."

"I know." I sniffled. "It was partly my fault. But she's supposed to be the grownup." I closed my eyes. "It's been a really hard day, Mom."

Mom held me a little tighter and stroked my hair with her other hand. "I stopped to check on Gram after work. She seemed to be doing a little better. She said you all visited this morning."

I nodded.

"I know you and Gram are really close."

I nodded again. "I don't want her to die."

122

"None of us do, Jada Jane. We'll be praying for her to get better."

I twisted around to look at Mom. "I didn't know you prayed. We never pray at meals like Gram does."

"Maybe we need to change that. I don't think I've done a very good parenting job in the spiritual department. We could all learn a lot from Gram." She kissed the top of my head. "Why don't you wash your face and come to dinner?"

"Okay." I wiped at my eyes again. Then I remembered what Kat and I had overheard outside an hour ago, though it seemed like ages had passed. "Mom, do you know why Lissa left her job in California?"

Mom looked confused. "Why does it matter? She told me she missed Oregon and that she wasn't getting along too well with her boss."

"Why not?"

"I don't know, JJ. I didn't ask. What brought this on?"

"Just curious."

Mom pushed herself up off the bed and gave me a hug. "See you in the kitchen in a few minutes. Dinner is about ready."

When I got out to kitchen, Lissa took a couple of hesitant steps toward me. Her eyes were red and her face a bit puffy. Had she actually been crying about it?

Wow, that was a surprise.

"JJ, I'm so sorry. Please forgive me."

Forgive her? After she broke my camera? I stiffened for a moment.

A picture of Gram popped into my head. She was holding a photo of our family and smiling like love itself—but with that tiny hint of sadness I sometimes saw in her eyes. Except for God, nothing mattered more to Gram than family. She had said to give Lissa a chance.

I grimaced and squeezed my eyes shut. Could I really forgive her? With my eyes closed, the picture of Gram got sharper, and she was staring straight at me. I couldn't bear that look. I opened my eyes and sighed. "Okay, I forgive you," I said, and I kind of meant it. "It was a little bit my fault too." I stumbled over and gave Lissa a quick hug.

She seemed surprised but hugged back.

It didn't help fix my camera, but somehow I felt a bit better. And I knew Gram would be happy.

Dad patted my head as he walked over to the table. "You can always ask for another one for Christmas. They're not that expensive."

Dad was so clueless sometimes. Cameras cost a lot and Christmas was six long months away. What would I do until then?

Now, more than ever, I needed a grand-prize winner. At least I already had a bunch of photos for the contest. One of my pictures had to be good enough. I wouldn't miss that old camera a bit once I had a shiny new DSLR. And I would make sure to find a much safer place to keep it than my nightstand.

I let that thought settle in my head, pushing away the doubt that tried to slip in. Yes, that was it. I would win. I had to! I slid into my chair, ready for dinner. Even if it was meatloaf.

After we'd eaten, Kat called. "Come over and hang out."

"Okay."

Kat let me right in when I walked over. Her mom waved from the living room, where she was watching some reality show, and I waved back. Then Kat and I headed for her room.

I sat on the purple bedspread.

Kat plopped down on the beanbag chair in the corner. "So, what happened with Lissa? Did she find out?"

I looked down at my shoes and took a deep breath. "Well, I think she was getting close, but then we had an argument, and my camera got broken. That kind of changed the subject."

"Oh no!" Kat clapped her hands to the sides of her face. She understood how much that camera meant to me, like a friend should. "You must have been raging mad."

"I was. But it was partly my fault. I threw a pillow at her, and she threw it back. But she hit the camera instead of me."

"Not cool. Not cool at all."

"No, not really." I looked at Kat. "At least I already uploaded the pictures I wanted at Ray's Camera Shop, plus I could use the memory card. And Lissa said she would take me to the shop tomorrow to see if they can fix it."

"What if they can't?"

I pressed my lips together and made my hands into fists. "I really have to win that grand prize. Or I won't have a camera until Christmas."

"Maybe Lissa would buy you a new one."

"Yeah, probably some cheapo thing way worse than

mine. I don't think she has much money right now."

Kat nodded several times. "Guess you're right. You have to win. Shouldn't be a problem, right? With all your talent." She grinned at me, and I tried to smile back.

That night when I went to bed, I said a prayer for Gram. I told God how much I needed Gram and asked Him to make her better. I lay there in the dark for a long time, waiting for an answer. But all I heard was the sound of cars in the distance and rain pattering on the roof.

19

When Lissa and I walked into Ray's Camera Shop, Mr. Browning smiled at me from his usual spot behind the cash register. "Come for your prints?" He reached under the counter, brought out a big envelope, and set it before me.

"Well, partly. I also have a problem."

"Oh, I'm sorry to hear that. Is it something I can help you with?"

I held out my camera. "It fell on the floor and broke. Do you think you can fix it?"

"I'll be paying for it," Lissa said.

Mr. Browning looked over at her and then back at me.

I remembered my manners. "Mr. Browning, this is my Aunt Melissa. Lissa, this is Mr. Browning."

Mr. Browning shook hands with Lissa, took my camera, and turned it around. He looked at the cracked screen, checked the lens, and toggled it to *On*.

Nothing.

He checked the batteries, then tried to turn it on again.

No luck.

He set the camera down. "Well," he said slowly. "I can't tell for sure whether it can be fixed. What I can tell is that it would cost more to fix it than the camera is worth."

I sighed. "I was afraid of that."

"With your talent, I recommend spending a little more and getting a better camera, one you can do more with."

I looked over at Lissa, raising my eyebrows in a question.

She shook her head. "I can't afford to buy you a better camera. I was hoping it could be fixed cheaply. Maybe your mom or dad could get you one."

"Maybe at Christmas." A painful, empty feeling sank into me. "I can't wait that long." I looked at the envelope on the counter. Was there any hope in those photos? "Mr. Browning, do you think any of those could win the grand prize at the fair? I really need that camera."

He opened the envelope and pulled out the photos, all nicely matted and ready to go. Latourell Falls, Kat, and the one of Lissa in the water. He stuck that one under the pile, tossing a glance at her.

"What was that one?" Lissa asked suspiciously.

"Not one of the better ones," Mr. Browning said, with a wink at me.

I liked him more all the time.

He came to the ones of Gram. "These are the best. I especially like the one of the hands. Powerful picture."

"Do you think it could win?"

He gave me an encouraging smile. "I can't tell, especially without seeing the other photographs that are entered. But I would say this one has a chance."

A bit of warmth crept into the emptiness inside me. "Thank you. I hope it does." I paused, looking at the picture with a piercing gaze. "It *has* to win."

Mr. Browning opened his mouth like he wanted to say something, but then he closed it again.

It *would* win, wouldn't it? It would be so great to beat out everyone else with Gram's picture. That news would probably make her feel lots better. I slid the photos back in the envelope and pulled out the last of my allowance money to pay for them. "I'll be back Thursday to pick up the others."

Maybe I could guilt Lissa into paying for them. Or Mom. And then I would be all set, except for taking them to the fair and filling out the entry forms. And waiting for the judges' decision. That would be the hardest part.

I trotted back to Lissa's car, hurrying to escape the light drizzle that was falling. Typical June day in Oregon—clouds, a bit of sunshine, some rain. I hoped the sun would come out later. Sunshine after the rain made for some beautiful pictures. Maybe there'd even be a rainbow.

Oh, wait. I wouldn't be taking any pictures today.

Ugh. No photos until at least Saturday, when the prizes would be awarded. At least that wasn't too far off.

I shoved my doubts back in a corner of my mind. It was going to be such fun getting to know my new camera. Such fun. "Can we go see Gram? I want to show her the pictures I took of her."

"Sure." Lissa's voice had a weird sound to it. "As long as you let me see that picture of me."

What? I gaped at her.

"I know the one Mr. Browning stuck under the pile so quickly had me in it. I just couldn't see what was going on." She sat there in the car, keys in hand, waiting. "Come on, out with it."

Reluctantly, very reluctantly, I pulled the incriminating photo out of the envelope, held it up briefly, and started to slide it back in.

Lissa grabbed the picture and studied it for a long moment.

I held my breath. What would she do? Scream? Tear up the picture?

Instead, she started chuckling.

Huh?

"Goodness, I look funny, don't I?"

I nodded.

"Really funny." She laughed a little harder.

"You sure do," I said, joining in the laughter.

"But I thought you erased that picture."

"I erased the picture you asked me to erase. But I had more than one. You only told me to erase *that* picture, not the rest."

Lissa snorted. "I forgot how sneaky kids can be." She handed the photo back to me. "Well, all I can say is, if that picture wins any money, you'd better split it with me."

"I can do that. But first, I have to figure out which category to enter it in—people or landscape. It has both."

"I would still prefer the garbage category."

When we arrived at Big Maples Retirement Home, the rain had stopped, at least for a bit. I grabbed the envelope with the photographs, leaving the broken camera in the glove compartment. We walked around a puddle by the front sidewalk and into the building.

A woman was standing in front of the reception desk.

Mom? Had she come to visit Gram during work? How odd. Cold fingers prickled my heart.

The receptionist looked over and saw me. Instead of her usual cheerful greeting, she turned and said something to Mom.

Mom spun toward us, her face pale and tight.

My heart stopped beating for an instant and then pounded like crazy. "Mom? Why are you here? Where's Gram? Is she okay?"

Mom looked at me with an empty expression. "I'm so sorry, JJ. She's gone."

"Gone?" What did she mean, gone? Where would Gram have gone? She couldn't mean ... No. I stared at Mom. "Where did she go?"

"No, Jada Jane. That's not what I meant. She's ..."

"Don't say it. I don't want to hear it." If she didn't say the words, then maybe it wouldn't be true. I would go up to Gram's room, she would smile at me like always, I would show her the pictures, and she would talk about my God-given gift.

"I'm sorry, Carol," Lissa murmured to Mom. "I hoped she would get better."

A fire tore through me but my hands felt icy.

Lissa put her hand on my shoulder.

I shook it off, took a step toward Mom ... but I couldn't move anymore.

She came over and put her arms around me, and I collapsed into them. "Oh, sweetie, I'm sorry. I'm so sorry." She held me close.

Wetness touched my cheeks. Was it from my tears

131

or Mom's? And why did it even matter? Why did *anything* matter?

Lissa leaned against Mom and patted my back.

This time I let her. "What happened?" I asked between sobs.

"She had a heart attack. They called an ambulance, but she died on the way to the hospital." Mom hugged me a little harder.

"But I still need her. It's not fair."

"Let's go home," Mom said. "Lissa, we'll meet you there."

I held Mom's hand like a little kid as we walked out to her car. Everything looked blurry, as if somebody threw water on a painting, and it was all dripping together into a big glob of gray.

When we got home, Dad and Brett were sitting at the kitchen table, grief in their eyes. Mom must have called home and told them already.

Mom and Lissa and I slumped down into the other chairs.

"You okay, sis?" Brett asked, his voice rough.

If I tried to talk, the words would turn into tears. Couldn't be a total baby in front of Brett and Dad.

Dad came over and gave me a little hug, then put his arms around Mom.

She grabbed hold of him and didn't let go.

"We'll have to go to the funeral home tomorrow and take care of things," he said after a couple of minutes.

Mom nodded. "I suppose so. I'll check with Big Maples and see if she had any plans set up. It would probably be easiest to do the service right at the funeral home."

"No!" I cried. It came out louder than I intended. Everyone turned to look at me. I took a breath and continued, more quietly. "We can't have the service at some funeral home. It has to be at Gram's old church, the one with the stained-glass windows."

Mom and Dad looked surprised.

"I suppose it would be nice to have it at her old church. But why is it so important to you?" Mom asked.

"That's what Gram would want. I know it is. I had a dream about that church, and I went there Sunday. The pastor still remembers Gram."

"You went there?" Mom stared at me, her mouth slightly open.

"Because of the dream. I wanted to see the stained-glass windows again." Did that make sense? Maybe not, but nothing made much sense.

Mom nodded, as if she understood. "I need to call the rest of the family."

"I'll call the church and find out when we can have the service," Dad said, taking his phone out of his pocket.

Good. They were listening to me. It had to be the way Gram would want. And yet it still seemed totally unreal. Like I would suddenly wake up and it would all be a nightmare that Mom would hug away.

I stumbled back to my room.

The door was open, and there, sleeping on my bed, lay Tasha. It was the first time she'd entered my room since Lissa moved in, almost like she knew I needed her.

I pulled the curtain closed and lay down on my bed,

my face against Tasha's soft fur. She purred quietly, and I petted her ever so gently, letting my world close in until Tasha and I made up our own little universe, protected and safe from all the hurt of the world.

20

Later that afternoon Mom brought a tuna sandwich and an apple to my room. "You need to eat something."

I tried, but the bread stuck in my throat and was hard to swallow. I ate a bit and gave some of the tuna to Tasha, whose appetite—especially for fish—was as good as ever. I called Kat and told her what happened. I kept it short, because my words threatened to turn into blubbering.

Kat would have understood if I'd broken down. I listened to her cry a lot when her dad left. Of course, she had been a little kid then. I was almost a teenager now.

Leaving Tasha on the bed, I headed down the hall. Mom and Dad were in the family room, quietly talking. Something about Grandma—which, of course, meant Gram—but the words were too quiet to make out. When I walked in, they stopped their conversation.

Mom quickly wiped her eyes, and Dad looked sad and solemn.

"How are you doing?" Mom asked. "Is there anything I can do for you?"

I shook my head. "I'm going over to the school to swing, okay?"

"Sure, JJ. That's fine." Mom looked at me like she used to when I was little and sick in bed, when she'd rub my back and make me feel better.

If only a backrub could bring Gram back.

"Let me know if you want to talk or anything," Mom said as I left the room.

Part of me wanted to, but the other part won out. I headed out the door, careful to close it behind me, then took off down the driveway and across the street to the school.

I jumped onto a swing and pushed off from the ground, pumping faster and faster. Higher and higher. I tried to swing high enough to escape into the clouds, but they kept pushing me back down to earth. I closed my eyes, feeling the wind on my face, the whip of my hair. Why did it still hurt so much inside?

A few raindrops fell, spattering like tears on my face. I kept pumping as hard as I could until my legs hurt. Finally, exhausted, I let the swing slow down on its own, then dragged my feet in the bark dust until I came to a stop, panting. I opened my eyes.

Kat sat quietly in the swing next to me.

I startled.

"Oh, didn't mean to scare you. You looked like you didn't want to be disturbed."

"I didn't," I said, "but it's okay. I'm done swinging."

"You were really moving."

"Yeah, but it didn't get me anywhere." I kicked at the bark dust. "I'm still right where I started, and nothing's changed."

"I'm going to miss Gram," Kat said. "I know I haven't seen her for a while, but we had fun when we were little and she babysat us. Remember how we played 'Hide and Seek' when she came over? We thought we were *so* good at it."

I laughed, but just barely. "Gram knew where we were all along. She probably wanted a few minutes of peace and quiet."

"Smart lady." Kat pushed herself back and forth a little in the swing. "And she would always bring animal crackers. A box for you and another box in case I came over."

I sat up a little straighter. "Do you remember the time I decided to climb the horse chestnut tree because I thought there was a bird's nest there? When Mom and Dad went out to dinner?"

"And you fell out, and we thought you broke your arm?"

"Poor Gram was so upset by my screaming that I felt sorry for *her*. I stopped crying and told her I was all right."

"And you were."

"But we didn't find that out for sure until Mom and Dad came home and took me to the emergency room. They had to leave in the middle of their dinner, and they weren't too happy with me because I knew I wasn't supposed to climb that tree."

"You always *were* kind of a brat," Kat said with a grin.

I threw some bark dust at her, but she grinned more. We sat quietly for a bit, looking out at the clearing clouds. Maybe we had some nice weather coming. It was getting near the end of June, so nice weather was about due.

"You believe in heaven, right?" Kat stared out at the clouds.

"Yeah."

"So then, Gram's okay, isn't she? She's probably dancing around heaven and having a great time."

Gram dancing? Yes, that would be like Gram. "I suppose so. But I wish she could still be here. Maybe *she's* having a great time, but I'm not."

"That's the bummer thing about it. We don't get to see her anymore."

I nodded.

"But at least you have pictures of her, right? You said you got some nice ones."

Yep. The photos would help me remember Gram. I sat up straight, and my eyes popped wide open. "Wait. Where are the pictures? What did I do with them?"

"Did you pick them up today?"

"I got them from Mr. Browning and took them to show Gram. But what happened to them after that? I don't remember bringing them in the house." I rubbed my forehead. "They must be in Mom's car. Come on. We have to go check." I jumped off the swing and ran for home. I got there before Kat, who greatly preferred walking to running unless tickling or dancing was involved, and rushed over to Mom's car.

It wasn't locked.

I opened the front door and climbed in. I checked the seats, the glove compartment—even though they wouldn't have fit there—and all of the floor.

No pictures.

"Maybe your mom took them in."

"Oh, that must be it."

We hurried up the steps and into the kitchen, where Kat closed the door carefully.

Mom was wiping off the counters.

138

"Mom, did you bring my photos in?"

She paused her cleaning. "Which photos?"

"The ones I had with me at Gram's. I don't remember what I did with them."

Mom shook her head. "I don't remember seeing any photos. Are you sure you had them?"

I nodded. "But I don't know what I did with them. I must have dropped them someplace." I gasped. "What if I dropped them in the parking lot there? If it rains, they'll be ruined. And those are my best pictures."

"I have to wait for a phone call right now," Mom said. "But I can take you over there later to look."

"I'll ride my bike." I was already halfway back out the door. "I need to go now."

Mom yelled her okay.

"I'll come." Kat hurried after me. "Let me get my bike too."

I pedaled hard down the bike lane, stopping at intersections to wait for the light to change—and for Kat to catch up. We reached the retirement home and parked our bikes. I stood there, glued to the concrete. My feet wouldn't move. Gram wasn't in there anymore. How could I bear the emptiness?

Kat grabbed my hand. "Come on. Let's go ask if someone found them and turned them in. Those pictures might be waiting for you right inside that door."

She pulled on my arm, and my feet came unglued. But it felt like they still stuck to the ground as I walked, and it was hard to keep going. Eventually, we made it to the receptionist's desk.

"Hey, JJ," the lady there said gently. "I'm so sorry about your great-grandma. She was really a special lady."

I nodded and looked at Kat.

"Ask her," she said.

I looked back at the receptionist. "I think I might have dropped a big envelope somewhere around here. It has some photographs inside. Very important photographs."

The lady frowned. "I don't recall seeing anything like that, but let me check." She opened drawers and filing cabinets and flipped through a pile of papers. "No, I don't see anything. Are you sure you dropped it here?"

I shook my head. "I'll look outside. Maybe I dropped it on the way to the car."

"I have your mom's phone number. I'll call if it turns up."

"Thanks." The place felt dark and ghostly, even with its bright lights and ivory-colored walls. I pushed open the door and escaped outside.

Kat and I walked through the entire parking lot twice, concentrating on the area where Mom had parked, but nothing was there.

I wilted onto the curb under one of the maple trees. My throat tightened, and my eyes stung. I hugged my knees and curled up as small as I could, trying to squeeze the pain away. I needed those photos—not just for the contest, but to remember Gram.

This was the lousiest day of my life.

"I don't know anyplace else to look." I took a ragged breath. "I know I had them here, and I didn't have them at home. They have to be around here somewhere."

"Maybe somebody picked them up and hasn't

turned them in yet. You'll probably get a phone call later, and they'll be fine."

"I hope so." But what were the odds? My luck hadn't been very good lately. Above me the clouds were breaking up, but inside my heart they were gathering, dark and stormy, and I felt helpless against them.

21

Nobody phoned that day, at least not about finding my photographs. Several relatives called, wanting to know what had happened and when the funeral would be and where they could stay if they came. Grandma and Grandpa would be driving up from California, along with Mom's brother and his wife and kids.

The next day Dad went back to work, but Mom didn't. She had to make arrangements at the funeral home and talk to the pastor about the service. No way was I going to the funeral home—there might be dead people in the back room. I knew Gram had to be there somewhere.

The church, however, was a different story. Lissa wanted to go too. Before we left, Mom agreed to call the retirement home again, in case my photos had turned up.

Still no pictures.

What was I going to do? Those were my best shot at the grand prize. Was it too late to order more? Why was everything so complicated? "Could we stop by Ray's Camera Shop?" I asked as we climbed into the car. "Maybe I could order more pictures. Except ..."

"Except what?" Mom asked.

"Except I think JJ's out of money and wants us to pay for them," Lissa said from the backseat.

I gave Mom my best pleading smile.

"I'll pay for them, JJ," Mom said. "I hope you can get them in time for the contest."

When we arrived, I ran into the shop first. "Mr. Browning, I need to order more pictures. I lost the ones I got yesterday." *God, please let there be time to order more. Please.*

"You lost them? That surprises me."

Mom and Lissa came up behind me. "Her great-grandma died yesterday," Mom explained quietly. "And I think they got dropped someplace."

Mr. Browning reached over and patted my hand. "I'm so sorry to hear that. Rose was such a wonderful lady. Yes, my dear, I think we can order more. Though it will cost extra for a rush order." He looked over at Mom and Lissa.

"That's fine," Mom said.

Fortunately, Mr. Browning still had the images saved, so I didn't have to see if my broken camera also had a broken memory card.

"I can have them for you tomorrow afternoon. Will that work?"

"I'll need to enter them on Friday, so that would be great." I let out a big breath. One day to spare. I could still win that contest, and Gram's picture would do it. It would be a fitting tribute to her. "I'll be in tomorrow afternoon to get them. Thank you very much."

We drove on to the little church with the stained-glass windows. I rushed over to the sanctuary.

The sun shone through the windows on one side, and they glowed like something heavenly. Was Gram on the other side looking in at me?

One window showed angels high above the ground,

hovering over baby Jesus in the manger. What would it be like to see real angels? Did they look like the ones in the window? If only I could ask Gram. She would know now.

"JJ," Mom called gently. "We need to talk to the pastor."

I followed Mom and Lissa to the church office.

Pastor Bob was there, talking with the secretary. He looked up and smiled. "Good to see you, although I wish it were under better circumstances." He took a few steps in my direction. "You're Rose's great-granddaughter, if I remember correctly." He held out a hand.

I shook it and my manners kicked in. "My name's JJ. And this is my mom, Carol, and my Aunt Lissa."

He showed us into his office and motioned toward some chairs that lined the room.

Mom settled into a seat. "We need to set up a service, but I don't really know what it should be like."

"Well, we do have a standard form we can follow. You only need to pick a couple of songs and a Bible verse."

Mom's expression still looked uncertain.

"And I can help you with that. I think I know how Rose would have liked it to be."

"Can we have 'What a Friend We Have in Jesus' for one song?" I asked. "Gram used to sing that to me when I was little, so I know she likes it."

"We certainly can." Pastor Bob lifted a notebook from his desk.

A grownup was actually listening to me again. Nice.

"And you said Sunday afternoon would be a good

time?" Mom asked.

Pastor Bob nodded. "That would be fine. Say, two o'clock?" The pastor leaned forward. "It would also help if you could write up something about her life for me to read, or at least refer to. I knew Rose, but I didn't know a lot about her before she came here."

"We can do that," Mom said.

"Be sure to say what a good artist she is ... was." I blinked a couple of times to clear my eyes.

Mom and Lissa set up the last details before we walked out to the car. The day was getting warm; maybe summer was finally arriving. I lifted my face to the sun, but its warmth didn't stop the cold throbbing inside.

"I need to swing by the retirement home to fill out some forms." Mom climbed into the car. "We'll have to empty out the apartment soon too, so they can rent it to someone else."

"What will happen to all of Gram's stuff?" I asked.

"We'll let family and friends choose a few things. Then we'll probably have a garage sale or something. And give the leftovers to charity."

"Even her paintings?" I pictured Gram's beautiful paintings hanging on the wall at Goodwill, on sale for $5.99. Lightning flashed through me. No, that couldn't happen.

"I think family will take most of those," Mom said. "I know I plan to keep a couple of them. Don't you think that big one she has in her living room would look good in our house?"

I tried to swallow the lump in my throat. "It would add some style."

"Our house could use some of that." Mom let out a single laugh. "In fact, while we're there, why don't we go up to the apartment and see if anything needs to be cleaned right away? We might get some food from the refrigerator before it goes bad. JJ, I'm sure there must be a couple of important things you would like, so you can have first dibs."

I looked out the window, pretending to watch the scenery. If I tried talking, the lump in my throat would choke me for sure.

Mom reached back and patted my leg as if she understood.

When we arrived at the retirement home, Mom stopped at the office to find out what she had to do and gave me the key to Gram's apartment.

Lissa headed toward the elevator, but I started up the stairs, so she turned around and followed me.

I was in no hurry to get there.

When we entered the apartment, it still looked and smelled the same. Newspapers were piled on the kitchen table, a couple of bowls and cups were in the sink, and the smell of lilac candles filled the air. Part of me wanted to run out of the room and never come back, but the other part wanted to touch everything that had belonged to Gram, as if that could somehow bring her back. I stood still in the middle of the living room.

Which of Gram's many special things did I want? What little pieces of her life would keep her memory fresh in my heart?

I wandered slowly through the small rooms, returned to the kitchen, got a paper grocery bag, and took it out to the living room. I put in the picture of Tasha and me and added a smaller painting that Gram had made of the ocean crashing against a rugged cliff, one skinny tree clinging to the top with its branches swept back by the wind.

Right now, I was that wind-battered tree.

Her bed was still unmade. I looked away and moved to the closet. An ivory-colored cardigan sweater hung in the back. Though it was old and very much out of style, Gram had worn it all the time in winter, and it smelled of her perfume.

I crammed it into my bag, walked over to Gram's bedside table, and picked up her Bible.

Inside the cover she had written the dates family members were born and the dates they died. It was like a family history, with God's Word holding it up. Nothing said Gram more than that.

I took the sweater out of the bag, wrapped it around the Bible, and placed the bundle back in my sack.

Lissa chose a painting and a couple of ceramic birds that she remembered from when she was a kid. "We should keep the rocking chair. Grandma spent a lot of time in that. I remember her rocking *you* in it when you were a baby."

Mom came in and moved from room to room, reaching out now and then to touch a picture, a piece of furniture, a knickknack.

What had Gram been like when she was thirty years younger? She must have really been energetic.

Mom opened Gram's desk, and an odd look settled on her face. "What's this?"

"What is it, Mom?"

"An envelope that says, 'Open this when I am gone.'"

Lissa and I moved closer. The crooked letters were definitely written by Gram's arthritic hand.

"Well," Lissa said. "We'd better take a look."

Mom opened the envelope and peeked inside. Then she pulled out one little key.

22

Mom turned the key over in her hand.

"What's it for?" I asked.

"It goes to her safety deposit box. I didn't know she still had it."

"What's a safety deposit box?"

"It's a locked container at a bank," Lissa said, sounding the slightest bit superior, "where people store valuables they want to keep safe, things they don't want to leave lying around at home."

"But why would Gram have one of those?" It didn't make sense. Gram didn't have any valuables besides her wedding ring, which she always wore, even though it'd been years since my great-grandpa died, and her paintings, which would need a pretty big box.

Mom shook her head. "That's what I asked her when she got it years ago. She had me go in and sign with her, so I could get access if something happened to her. But she never said why she wanted it." Mom put the key back in the envelope and stuck the envelope in her purse. "Well, I'll get to the bank Friday and see what's in the box. I doubt it's very much. It isn't like Gram was rich or anything."

"I think she was rich," I said, "just not money-rich."

"You're right, JJ." Mom reached out and gave me a one-armed hug. "Well, let's clean out the refrigerator and get home. I've got a lot to do to get ready for the

149

memorial service on Sunday. And I still have my class tomorrow and a paper due Friday."

That afternoon, after Mom worked on her paper, she and Lissa drove to the funeral home to finish "making arrangements," as she said.

Brett returned from working the lunch shift at the burger place and headed to his room.

The quiet house pressed in around me. I couldn't sit still, so I called Kat and invited her over. We settled into the couch in the family room, Tasha between us, and I told Kat about the discovery of the key.

"Ooh!" She squirmed in her seat. "Another mystery. What could she have hidden away in that little box? Which riches were so important she had to put them in the bank?"

"I don't think Gram had any riches of that kind." I frowned and kicked at the rug. What *could* it be?

"Maybe rare jewels sent by a secret lover." Kat winked.

I shook my head. "You know Gram did *not* have a secret lover. She wasn't that kind of person."

"Maybe old coins, passed on from generation to generation and now worth a small fortune." She smiled as if she was really pleased with that idea.

"I don't know. Maybe, but probably not."

"Or stocks that she bought as a young lady and that are now worth millions."

"Not too likely. If Gram had a million dollars, she would've shared it."

Kat sighed. "You're no fun. Come on, think of something wonderful and mysterious that might be in there."

I laughed. "I have no idea what it could be. We'll have to wait until Friday to find out."

"Your family is full of mysteries. What Gram has in her safety deposit box … why Lissa got fired …"

"Lissa got fired?" Brett's voice came from the doorway.

I jerked my head around. When had he walked in? I glared at Kat.

"Oops," Kat said in a small voice.

"How do you know Lissa got fired?" Brett scratched his head. "I thought she quit 'cause she wanted to move back up here."

"No, she got fired. For sure." Kat nodded. "We saw the email."

"Kat!" I cried.

She shrugged. "It's too late. The cat's out of the bag." She gave Tasha a pat. "So to speak."

Brett rubbed his chin. "Wow, I never would have guessed. No wonder she didn't find a place to live first. She probably didn't have time."

"Don't say anything, Brett. Please." Clasping my hands, I begged him. "We'll get in trouble for snooping."

"You don't snoop in *my* room, do you?" His eyes narrowed.

I shook my head. "Of course not. I value my life."

Brett grinned. "Good point. Okay, I won't say anything. I just hope Lissa doesn't find out. I have a feeling she would be pretty unhappy about it." Brett glanced at the clock and waved at us. "See you later. I'm off to practice. Don't do anything I wouldn't do." He headed for the door.

"That leaves it wide open!" Kat hollered after him.

Brett looked back and grinned again.

I turned back to scowl at Kat. Why couldn't she keep her mouth shut? "What if Brett changes his mind and tells Mom? Or it sort of slips out?"

Kat gave a sheepish grin. "Sorry. How was I supposed to know he was standing there?"

I slumped back against the couch. Life was one thing after another, as Mom sometimes said. She had a point.

"How long do you think it will be before your mom and Lissa are back?"

"I don't know. Maybe an hour," I muttered. "Why?"

"I think it's our duty to find out why she was fired. And this is our chance. We have the house to ourselves. How often does that happen?"

"Pretty often, actually. And don't you think one close call a day is enough?"

"Nobody else is home to sneak up on us," Kat said. "It's not like we're doing any *new* snooping. We'd merely be finishing up what we started the other day. What if she got fired for stealing? She could be swiping things from your mom and dad without them even being suspicious."

I hesitated. Gram would have said Lissa was family, to give her a chance. But what if Kat was right? We would be protecting my family by finding out. "I don't know …"

Kat jumped up. "That sounds like an almost-yes to me. Close enough. Let's go." She trotted down the hall toward my room.

I followed because I had to—or at least that was my

excuse. But what would Gram think? And what would Mom say if she found out?

By the time I got there, Kat already had Lissa's email open. "We need to find work email. Or maybe email to her boyfriend. What's his name?"

"Thomas. I don't know his last name."

Kat scrolled through the email. She stopped and opened one. She scrunched up her face. "Ooh, gushy stuff in this one. Lovey-dovey and all that. But nothing about her job." She clicked it closed and kept looking.

"Maybe we should go." Invisible bugs climbed all over me and prickled my skin. *Hurry up, Kat!*

"Nah, we can't quit. Something's bound to turn up. What was her boss's name?"

"I haven't the slightest idea. I don't even know the name of the company."

Kat snorted. "Well, you're not much help."

Down the hall, the back door creaked open.

Oh no. "Kat, somebody's home!"

"It's probably Brett," she said. "I didn't hear a car."

"Get off the computer," I snapped. "We can't take a chance."

Footsteps started down the hall.

Kat looked up, eyes wide. She clicked the *X* on the email window and jumped up from the computer, knocking over the chair.

"Kat!" I hissed. I motioned toward the chair and stepped into the hall.

Lissa walked slowly toward me, shoulders drooping. She wore her tight jeans with a dark top—and plain sneakers for a change.

"What are you doing home?" I tried to keep my

153

voice calm. "I didn't hear the car."

"Your mom had some shopping to do, so I decided to walk home. I needed the exercise."

Kat slipped out of the room. "Hi, Lissa." She smiled up at my aunt, looking angelic. Or as angelic as Kat could.

Lissa's eyes narrowed. "What are you guys up to? You have guilt written all over your faces."

"That's not guilt," Kat quipped. "Probably peanut butter from lunch."

Lissa strode into the room and looked around. She glanced around the desk and her eyes locked on the computer screen. "My computer should be in sleep mode. I haven't used it for hours. But my desktop is up." She wheeled around to look at us. "What have you been doing?"

"I think I need to go home," Kat said. "Time to fix dinner for Mom." She waved and hurried down the hall.

What a coward! Deserting me in my time of need—again. And leaving me alone with an irate aunt who seemed to be figuring things out.

Lissa stared at me, hands on hips. "Okay, kid, what's the story? Have you been getting into my stuff?"

"We didn't do much. Really. I'm sorry." *Please, please, don't ask.*

"Sorry?" Lissa's voice rose. "Sorry? That's not good enough. Why were you messing with my computer?"

I took a deep breath. Might as well come clean, scary as that was. "Kat thought you might have some good secrets. And then we found out you were fired. And we wanted to find out why."

"Fired? What makes you think that?" Her voice

practically squeaked, and her cheeks turned red.

"Kat saw an email."

"You had no right to look at my email. That's private, and it's none of your business." She shook her head, eyes dark and mouth tight. "And I thought we could be friends. I guess that's not going to happen."

Why hadn't I listened to Gram? My stomach turned to concrete, and I stuck my hands into my pants' pockets to keep them from shaking. Yet that question still nagged at me: why *was* she fired? "Well," I blurted out, "you weren't honest with us either. You said you quit your job because you wanted to move back to Oregon. But that's not true, is it?"

Her face got redder. She walked to the window and stood there, looking out, for a long minute. When she walked back and sat in her chair, her face was blank.

Did that mean she was getting over it—or that she was mad beyond words? The tension was breaking that concrete inside me into sharp chunks. I pressed a hand against my tummy.

Lissa rolled her chair over and grabbed the end of the curtain, pulling it shut between us. "Go away," she growled from behind the curtain. "I don't want you around right now."

Probably not the best time to remind her that this was actually *my* room. I plodded to the family room, picked Tasha up from the couch, and sat down, settling her into my lap. She purred and rubbed her head against my hand as I petted her. Gloom settled over me.

Why had I listened to Kat? What a mistake.

Now what? I was in trouble with Lissa, and I would be in trouble with Mom as soon as she found out. I was kicked out of my own room with nowhere to go. And I couldn't even call Gram and complain to her.

Of course, in this case, she would be on Lissa's side anyway.

I sat and held Tasha until Mom came home.

She made a couple of trips back out to the car, thumping bags of groceries down on the counter. After the last bag, she glanced toward the family room. When Mom saw me, her face got that worried look of hers. "What's the matter, JJ?"

"I kind of had a fight with Lissa," I said. Should I tell her about it? Would I be in more trouble if I told or if I didn't?

"Want to talk about it?"

I shook my head. "Not really."

"Well …" Mom tilted her head to the side. "Maybe I'll go talk to Lissa. Can't have people fighting in this house."

Great. Mom would hear Lissa's side of it first, and I wouldn't even be there to defend myself. But then, how could I defend myself when I was the guilty one?

23

I stumbled into the kitchen and started putting groceries away. Maybe Mom wouldn't be quite as mad if I at least did something helpful. I finished, but she was still in my room with Lissa.

They were talking a long time. Was that good or bad?

My stomach knotted up and my hands felt sweaty. I wiped them on my pants and looked down the hall.

When I was little and did something wrong, Dad would usually swat me on the bottom. It hurt a bit, but it was over almost before I knew it, and I could go back to playing.

Mom, however, would sit me in a chair and tell me to think about what I had done while she decided on the punishment. I sat there imagining all the things that Mom might do. Would she ground me for a week? Take away a favorite toy? Make me do a million chores? The possible penalties grew bigger and bigger in my mind while I waited.

My fears always turned out to be worse than reality, and the waiting was usually the hardest part of the punishment. But that never stopped me from worrying the next time I messed up.

Dad's car rattled into the driveway, and a car door slammed. He walked into the kitchen, carrying his lunch bag. He glanced around the room and sniffed the air, looking a bit disappointed. "Where's your mom? I'm hungry."

"Back talking to Lissa."

"Okay." He looked around again, then seemed to actually see me. "How was your day?"

"Could have been better."

Dad nodded. "It's a hard time for everyone. I'll go change, and then we can find out what Mom has in mind for dinner."

Good ol' clueless Dad.

While he was changing, Mom emerged from the bedroom.

I stiffened. Now what?

Mom said, "Lissa wants to talk to you."

"Am I in trouble?" I studied Mom's face for a sign of what might be awaiting me, but I couldn't read it.

"That's up to Lissa."

I plodded back to the bedroom, moving as slowly as possible. When I entered the room, Lissa was sitting in her chair, and my chair was in front of hers.

She motioned for me to sit down, her expression as hard to read as Mom's.

I sat and waited, feeling like the slightest touch might make me explode. My legs wanted to move—to race outside and down the street until they couldn't take another step—but I held them still. My breath came in short little bursts.

Finally, after what seemed like an hour but was probably only a minute, Lissa spoke. "It really hurt me to find out I couldn't trust you. I know it's hard having to share your room, but I honestly thought we might be friends."

My eyes felt itchy. "I'm sorry. I know it was wrong to spy on you."

"Kat talked you into it, didn't she?"

Kat was my best friend, but she didn't always have the greatest ideas. And it was rotten of her to run off when we got caught. Couldn't I let her take the blame? I was an innocent bystander, right? I could almost see Gram frowning. I swallowed. "It wasn't all her fault. I could have made her stop."

"I know. I was really mad at you at first, but your mom and I had a long talk. I realized I hadn't been fair to you guys. I didn't trust your family with the truth about why I left California, and I should have."

I relaxed the teensiest bit. Maybe I wasn't in as much trouble as I had feared. Was I going to find out Lissa's deep, dark secret?

"You were right about one thing. I *was* fired. But it wasn't my fault. My supervisor tried to get me to do something wrong, so he could get more money. But I wouldn't do it. So he made up a story about me and fired me."

Wow. My jaw dropped. Kat and I had never even thought of anything like that. "If it was wrong, why didn't you go to the police?"

"The supervisor said, if I told anyone, he would make sure I never got another job in the industry. Thomas tried to talk me into telling someone, but I was afraid."

A tiny light bulb lit up in my head. So *that* was what the telephone conversation we overheard had been about. Not about her getting arrested, but about her turning someone in. And we had totally misinterpreted it. "I'm sorry, Lissa. That must have been horrible."

She fiddled with the computer mouse. "It was. Devastating. But then I thought about coming back up here. I love Oregon, and I thought it might be nice to live near you guys. I figured maybe I could turn something bad into something good."

"Kind of like making lemonade if someone hands you lemons."

"Exactly. And if I can ace the interview tomorrow, I'll be making a good start. Next, I have to work on getting Thomas to move up here."

My legs settled down, and my stomach began to unknot. "So you aren't totally mad at me anymore?"

She shook her head. "How about I forgive you, and you forgive me? We'll start fresh."

I nodded. Whew. I could breathe again.

She pointed at me and narrowed her eyes. "But if you ever do it again, I'll skin you alive."

My eyes popped open wide.

Lissa winked.

I slumped down in my chair as the rest of the tension drained out. "I guess you can be as dangerous as Brett. I'll be careful."

Lissa held out her arms, and I leaned forward and gave her a hug.

Jumping to conclusions wasn't such a good idea after all. Things weren't always as they seemed.

Lissa stood and stretched. "Did you bring a painting home from Gram's?"

"Yes, I did." I went over to my bed, grabbed the bag, and pulled the painting out. "I got this one with the ocean."

"Ooh, nice. Let me show you the one I chose." She picked up a big package wrapped in newspaper and pulled the papers off. It was the painting that had hung over Gram's bed, of a path through the woods. The sun was shining through the trees, lighting the path.

As a little kid, I'd wanted to follow that trail. It had to lead to someplace secret and special. "I like that one too."

Lissa walked over to the wall and took down two of her abstract pictures. "I think Gram's paintings should go here, don't you?"

I reached up to hang mine, while Lissa put hers on the other nail. They looked really nice on our wall.

Maybe Lissa wasn't that bad. She had done the right thing in a hard situation. Lots of people would have obeyed the supervisor to keep the job, but she didn't. Maybe Gram was right about her.

In my mind I framed a picture of Lissa standing next to Gram's paintings. It would be called *Aunt Melissa*—because she was actually starting to feel like my aunt. But I had no way to take that picture.

I missed my camera.

Before dinner I ran over to Kat's house and told her everything was okay.

"What a relief." She wiped her forehead with the back of her hand. "I was afraid I'd be banned for life."

"No, but I think your life as a spy needs to end."

Kat put on a big frown. "Really? I had a real future there. Then again …" She struck a pose with one hand on her hip and the other up in the air, hand bent downward. "I think my real calling is acting, after all. And I've never heard of an actress-spy."

161

"Well, spies do have to be good at acting."

Her eyes lit up.

What was I saying? I wasn't too fond of Kat as a spy. "But spies have to do it in secret, you know. They never become famous."

Kat posed again. "Acting it is!"

I headed home for dinner. Mom had decided on fajitas, something quick but delicious. We were all pretty happy … as long as we didn't think about Gram. As if that were even possible.

For some reason I woke up early the next morning and heard my parents both take off for work. I lay in bed for a while, thinking about the photographs I would pick up that day. Once I got them, I would lay everything out and plan which ones to enter. One or two in every category would give me the best chance to win. Maybe more in the people category. I would enter a picture of Kat, as well as those of Gram. Didn't want to hurt Kat's feelings.

On the other side of the curtain, Lissa climbed down from her bunk and started up her computer. Her interview was at two o'clock, and she was probably nervous, hoping they didn't ask too much about her last job.

I looked over at Gram's paintings. They looked good on the wall. When I got my room back, I wanted to have Gram's pictures on one wall and my best photographs on another.

Thinking of Gram made me remember the key

Mom found. Whatever could Gram have in a safety deposit box? If only Mom had time to get to the bank today, the mystery could be solved.

Lissa left the room.

I leaned down and picked up the bag I'd brought home from Gram's. I unwrapped the sweater from the Bible and ran my hands over the soft patterns of the yarn. I held it against my face and smelled Gram's perfume. If I closed my eyes, I could almost feel her hugging me.

I picked up the Bible. Gram had always kept it with her. She read it every night at bedtime and every morning before she even got up. Something that important to her was probably worth reading. But where should I start?

There were bookmarks in a few places.

Perhaps those were her favorite parts. I would start with them.

The first marked Psalm 139. The number was circled with ink. "O Lord, thou hast searched me, and known me."

Thou and *hast* threw me for a minute, but I got the idea. God knew me. Gram said God believed in me, so I guess He had to know me. The psalm said I couldn't hide from God, but it didn't seem to mean the kind of hiding when I'm in trouble and didn't want Mom to find me. It seemed more like a good thing, like God would always be with me, no matter what.

The words of the psalm sang like music. They talked about the thoughts of God and ended with "lead me in the way everlasting."

The way everlasting. That was the path Gram had

walked. It was almost like she was there watching me read, wrapping her arms around me in love.

I gently closed the Bible and set it on my nightstand. Later I would read the next bookmarked place, but right now I had enough to think about.

I kept checking the clock that morning, waiting for afternoon to arrive, so I could pick up my photographs. I was curious to see how the ones with Brett came out—and eager to get the ones of Gram replaced.

Lissa spent the morning fussing around—taking a shower, doing her hair, filing her fingernails. She really wanted to look her best for the interview. After lunch she worked on her make-up. It had to be "subtle but effective."

Whatever worked, I guess. If it helped her get the job, I was all for it.

When Lissa left, I took off for Ray's Camera Shop with some money Mom had left. I pedaled, wearing my backpack so I'd have a way to carry the pictures home.

The sky was still gray, but it hadn't started to rain yet. Perhaps it would hold off for another day or two. Sunshine would be nice for the fair. Mom had said she would take Kat and me Saturday to go on the rides until the photography contest winners were announced. Woohoo!

The sun broke through the clouds for a moment, sending those long rays shooting down to earth like light from heaven. This time it seemed extra-special, because I knew someone in heaven.

My throat burned, and I swallowed back tears. I clicked the camera in my mind and hoped the picture would last.

As soon as I entered the shop, Mr. Browning handed me the photos. "I wish you all the best in the contest."

"I have to win." I reached into my pocket for the money. "It feels so weird not having a camera. I see things I want to take pictures of but can't. The memory I try to keep isn't the same."

Mr. Browning tapped the counter. "I know what you mean. You definitely have the photography bug. And I'm afraid there's no cure. For the rest of your life, you'll be seeing photographs in everything you look at."

"Really?" That sounded wonderful. "I hope so."

Laughing, Mr. Browning handed me my change. "See you at the fair."

"Wait, you'll be there?"

"Of course." He chuckled. "I'm always watching for new talent—and customers for my classes. Again, good luck!"

I smiled, thanked him, put the envelope in my pack, and pedaled toward home.

Did I have the winner?

Oh, please, God, please!

24

When I got back from the camera shop, Lissa's car was already in the driveway. Was that a good sign or a bad one? She hadn't been gone very long, but maybe it didn't take the business long to decide. Still, if she had bad news, it could wait.

After putting my bike in the garage, I sat down at the picnic table in the backyard. I spread the pictures out in front of me, studying each one carefully.

The two of Gram would definitely be entered. Even Mr. Browning had said they were good. Brett and his teammate looked so energetic and joyful that I had to enter that one in the sports category.

I slid those back into the envelope and considered the rest.

The next one was Lissa falling in the water. Did the judges like humor? It should get points for that. But how would I feel if someone entered a picture of me falling on my rear?

Could be embarrassing.

Okay, forget it. I slid it into the envelope at the bottom of the pile.

Maybe the two waterfall pictures?

The back door burst open and Lissa flew out, still wearing her black skirt and white blouse, face glowing.

Could it be? I held my breath.

"I got the job!" she cried. "They hired me! I start

work on Monday." She danced around the picnic table, a tricky feat with those high heels. Pure joy shone on her face, and she wobbled around crazily.

Where was a camera when I needed it? I jumped up and raised my hand for a high-five.

She slapped it with hers and grabbed for my hands, trying to get me to dance with her.

I fell back onto the bench and grinned, hiding my hands behind my back so she couldn't reach them. She was acting a bit too weird for me. "Good job. I mean, good thing you *got* the job."

"I'm so happy," she practically sang. "They didn't ask anything about my last job, so I didn't have to explain things. And they seem like really nice people. I can't wait to tell your folks."

"They'll be so happy for you too." Especially Dad. But not as happy as me.

I pictured my room back to normal, with Tasha asleep on my bed and my photographs on the wall—along with Gram's paintings, of course. A warm glow spread through me.

Lissa spun again, all the way to the back door.

The *open* back door.

"Lissa, you left the door open."

"Oops. I was so excited I forgot." She stopped dancing, and her forehead wrinkled. "I think I closed it when I came home. But maybe not."

"Lissa!" How could she have forgotten *again*?

"I know," she said. "We don't want Tasha to get out. Don't worry. I'll close it now and check to make sure Tasha is still inside, safe and sound."

"Okay." I turned back to my photos. When would

she ever learn? At least she would be moving out soon.

Lissa went into the house and closed the door. Her voice echoed through the house and out to me as she called for Tasha.

Silly. Did she think Tasha would come running to *her*? Cats were way pickier than that.

A few minutes later the door flew open again, but this time panic covered Lissa's face.

I jumped up. "You didn't find Tasha?"

"I looked all over. And then I looked out the front window, and I saw a cat crossing the street. I think it was her."

"*Lissa!*" I screamed. "How could you?"

Her face looked all apologetic, but that didn't help.

"I told you to keep the door closed." How could she have been so stupid?

Now Tasha was out in an unfamiliar world, lost and scared. What if a dog got her?

"She can't have gotten too far," Lissa said. "Hurry. Let's go check where I saw the cat cross the street."

I ran out to the road, heart pounding, then slowed down to check for traffic. I had to stay calm and quiet. A lot of commotion might scare Tasha into hiding.

Lissa followed me, trying to hurry in those ridiculous high heels.

"Tasha," I called softly. "Here, kitty, kitty. Tasha." I looked over at Lissa. "Where did you see the cat go?"

Lissa pointed between two houses. "But we can't walk into someone's yard. That's trespassing."

"You ask permission. I'm going to look for Tasha." I crept along the side of the house, calling quietly and watching for any movement.

Lissa actually did go knock on the door, but nobody answered. She joined me as I inched toward the backyard.

"Tasha." I called louder, but still found no sign of her. "This is where you saw her go?"

Lissa nodded. "But I don't see her now."

That was obvious. My insides felt like snakes were slithering all around them. And my heart pounded so hard it made my head hurt. "We need help." I ran across the street and knocked on Kat's door.

She opened the door a moment later. "Hi, JJ, what's going on?"

"Tasha got out. Can you help look for her?"

"Sure. I found her last time, didn't I?" She grabbed a jacket and rushed out to join Lissa and me.

The three of us walked up and down the street, looking in yards and calling.

Rain started to fall, a drop here and a drop there at first, but getting heavier by the minute.

"Maybe she went home while we were out looking." Lissa rubbed her arms. "She might be howling at the back door right now."

"Maybe," I said. "Let's go look." We headed back, stopping to check at the front door first.

No cat there. Around to the back door. Still no cat. But the rain pounded down, thick and hard.

"Inside, girls," Lissa said. "We'll look some more when the rain lets up."

I glanced around the backyard one last time before heading inside—and then I saw them.

My photographs sitting on the picnic table, dripping with rain.

25

I raced over to the picnic table and grabbed the envelope, along with the few photographs that had been out in the open, then ran for the house.

Kat and Lissa were drying themselves off with kitchen towels when I came in. I must have looked even more panicked than before, because Kat stopped toweling off her hair and stared at me.

"What's wrong?" she asked. "Besides the obvious, I mean."

I held out the package. "My photographs. They're all wet." I bit my lip to stop its quivering. First Tasha and now this. I threw the loose photos down on the table.

They were totally mushy and useless. Blues and greens and grays all smeared together like a toddler's finger painting.

My body felt full of lead weights. I blinked back tears.

"Maybe the ones in the envelope are all right." Lissa grabbed a fresh towel and wiped the outside of the package. She took some paper towels and went over it again. "Now dry yourself off before you open it."

I dried my hands and my hair enough that I wouldn't drip—and gave my eyes a quick wipe—sat at the kitchen table, and carefully opened the envelope.

Lissa and Kat leaned over, silently waiting.

I pulled out the stack of pictures. "No!" The one on top had a wet smear across it. I laid them out, one at a time, across the table.

The pictures of Brett had been in the middle and only had a little water damage to the cardboard mats. They would be usable. The rest were totally ruined, including the ones of Gram.

Lissa's eyes narrowed a bit when she saw the picture of herself in the water, but only for a moment. She looked back at me, tears in her eyes. "Oh, JJ, I'm so sorry. It's all my fault."

"Yeah, it is," I growled, a volcano getting ready to erupt inside me. "I've lost the contest, and I've lost my cat, and it's all your fault." I stormed back to my room and threw myself on the bed. I pounded my fists into the pillow and screamed.

Why did everything have to go wrong? My whole world was falling apart. First Gram died—the worst thing of all—then I lost the pictures, then Tasha ran away, and now my other pictures were ruined.

God, where are You? Do You hate me this much?

Rain pelted against the window.

Tasha.

I gave one last scream and jumped up from the bed. I couldn't save the pictures, and I couldn't bring back Gram, but I could still look for Tasha. A little rain wasn't going to stop me. I grabbed my rain jacket and headed down the hall.

Kat and Lissa were still in the kitchen, looking lost themselves.

"I'm going to look for Tasha." I zipped up my jacket.

"I'll go get my umbrella," Kat said and ran out the door.

"Let me change." Lissa patted her wet skirt. "I can't look for a cat in heels."

I shook my head. "You stay here in case Tasha comes back." Lissa helping right now was *not* a good idea. I would probably either hit her or call her names I'd get in trouble for. I headed out the door without waiting for an answer. "We have to think like a cat," I said when Kat joined me. "Where would a cat go in the rain?"

"I'm good at thinking like a Kat."

"Tasha could fit into little places, hard-to-find places. I just wish I knew how far she went. Or in which direction. Lissa isn't even sure the cat she saw was Tasha." I looked at the gray, wet street. "Let's start close to home and gradually go farther away."

"We should start in your yard, then."

I nodded. We checked the front yard, the sides, and the back, looking under every bush, behind the garage … in every nook and cranny, as Mom would say. We searched around Kat's house next. That was where Tasha had ended up last time, so it seemed like a logical place to look.

Nothing.

We kept going, but couldn't find Tasha anywhere. She had never wandered off like this before. Where could she have gone?

When we were a few houses down, I heard someone calling my name. It sounded like Mom.

"Maybe Tasha is home," I cried. "Let's go see." We ran down the street, rain slapping our faces, feet

172

splashing through mud puddles. We slowed down as we neared my place.

Kat pointed at her driveway. "My mom's car. I have to go check-in because I didn't have time to leave a note. Let me know if you need more help."

"Thanks." I waved and ran up the driveway and into the kitchen.

Dinner was on the table. Brett was already eating, and everyone else was dishing up chicken, potatoes, and beans. Was it really that late?

"Oh, JJ, I'm glad you heard me. It's time to eat."

"Did Tasha come home?" I glanced from face to face.

Lissa looked down at her plate.

"Not yet," Mom answered. "But I'm sure she will. She's just hiding from the rain."

"I can't eat until Tasha's home. I need to keep looking."

"Sit down," Mom said firmly. "But first, hang up that dripping jacket." She looked at me more closely. "If you want energy to hunt, you need to eat."

I groaned but hung up my jacket and sat down. I tried to eat, but the potatoes stuck in my throat, and the chicken took forever to chew. And the green beans were too green.

"I'm really sorry," Lissa said. "I'll help you look after dinner."

I didn't say anything. As Mom liked to remind me, if I couldn't say something nice, I shouldn't say anything at all. And I couldn't say anything nice to Lissa yet.

After dinner Mom apologized for not being able to help, but said she had to finish that paper before bed.

Brett left for baseball practice—held in the school gym, due to the rain. Dad searched the yard, then went inside, saying he would be listening if Tasha came back and meowed at the door.

Probably a baseball game on TV.

Kat and I searched some more. Lissa went in the opposite direction as if she knew I didn't want her around me. The rain had eased some. Maybe Tasha would come out from wherever she was hiding. But there was still no sign of her. We even knocked on a few doors and asked if anyone had seen a black cat with white on its chest, but no one had.

When it started getting dark, we headed home. If we couldn't find her in the light, there was no way we would be able to find her at night.

I sat at the kitchen table after everyone but Mom had gone to bed, hoping Tasha would suddenly show up at the back door, scratching and yowling with hunger. I laid my head down to rest for a minute. I woke to Mom rubbing my back, and sat up. "Is Tasha back?" I glanced around the kitchen with bleary eyes.

"Not yet, but it's eleven thirty, and you need to go to bed."

"But I have to be here to let Tasha in if she comes back."

Mom pointed down the hall.

When I got back to my bedroom, Lissa was still up.

"No cat yet?"

I shook my head and closed the curtain between our beds.

"I'll go and keep an ear out for her," Lissa said through the curtain.

The bedroom door closed quietly.

I was still mad at her, but a little less than before. She was trying her best to make up for her mistake. And she wasn't the first person to ever leave the door open. I had even done it once myself. Gram would tell me to forgive her, but that was hard to do with Tasha still missing.

Before going to bed, I took another look at my pictures. Mom had laid them on my desk. They were dry now but still as ruined as ever. Only two were any good at all, and even those had a bit of damage to the mats. I did have some pictures from the very first batch—the view from the top of the school, an old building, a big maple tree, and one of Kat. But even Gram hadn't thought those had a chance at winning the grand prize.

God, please help me. I don't know what to do. Help me find Tasha. If You want me to win that contest, I'm going to need a miracle. But right now, I want Tasha to come home. I climbed into bed. *And, God, please tell Gram I miss her.*

It was after midnight when I fell asleep, and I had horrible dreams of Tasha floating away down a flooded street and the judges laughing at my smeared photographs.

26

"Wake up, sleepyhead."

I lifted my head off the pillow and blinked. Light streamed through the window, so it couldn't be too early. Why did I feel so groggy?

It all came back to me. Tasha … the photos … the big mess that life had become …

"Are you awake?" Lissa's voice again.

"Is Tasha back?" I swung my feet out of bed and rubbed my eyes.

"No, but I'm going to look for her. Want to come?"

"Of course." I jumped out of bed. "What time is it?"

"Almost eight."

Yikes! How could I have I slept so late when Tasha was still missing? I yanked on a pair of jeans and a T-shirt.

When I emerged from my side of the room, Lissa handed me a granola bar. "Here, have some breakfast and let's get going." Lissa led the way to the kitchen. "Your folks left for work. And it's stopped raining, so it'll be easier to search for the cat." She paused by the back door. "I wish we had some magic way to find her. A cat magnet or something."

My eyes opened wide. Light finally reached my brain. "A cat magnet? Why didn't I think of that yesterday?"

"Huh?" Lissa narrowed her eyes. "You actually have a cat magnet?"

I opened the cupboard that held the canned cat food. Chicken and liver, beef, turkey. Ah, here it was: tuna, Tasha's favorite. I turned toward Lissa and held out the can, so she could see the label.

"Ah, now I get it."

"It worked before when Tasha got scared once and hid behind the washing machine. Maybe it will work again." I opened the can, grabbed a spoon, and wrinkled my nose at the fishy smell. Would it be strong enough to bring a hungry cat out into the open?

Lissa and I headed outside. The sun had broken through the clouds, which were slowly dissolving into the blue. It might be a nice day.

I spooned a clump of food onto the top step, then a couple of smaller chunks leading up to it. I dropped a little more in the driveway. "I hope Tasha smells it before the other neighborhood cats do." I walked around the yard, holding the open can down near every bush and up near every tree. "Tasha!" I called. "Come here, Tasha!"

We walked down the street a bit.

A meow!

My heart pounded. Tasha?

But it was just a neighbor's cat, attracted by the tuna.

I dumped a little on the ground, so it wouldn't follow us. "Let's check where you thought you saw her, Lissa. Maybe she's still there—if that was her."

We crossed the street and came to the place.

"Tasha. Here, kitty, kitty, kitty. Tasha!" I stopped to listen and crouched down with the tuna can.

Lissa stood next to me, not saying a word.

"Murrr …"

What was that sound? Could it be? *Please, God, please let it be Tasha!* "Here, Tasha. Here, kitty!" I stuck the spoon into the tuna and lifted up a big chunk.

Something moved in the bushes to the right of us. A dark shape glided through the leaves.

"Tasha?"

"Merow."

Was that dirty cat with wet fur pasted to its body really Tasha? I held my breath. *Please!*

The cat trotted over, rubbed against my legs, and dove for the food.

Yes, definitely Tasha! Fireworks burst inside me, glorious sparkling fireworks. I giggled like a first grader. My cat had returned.

Lissa crouched down, covered her face with her hands, and swiped at her eyes. "That's the most beautiful cat I've ever seen."

"If you think she's beautiful this minute, you'd better see an eye doctor." I kept petting Tasha as she ate.

Lissa gave me a gentle nudge.

I could probably forgive her now. I let Tasha eat a bit, then gave the cat food can to Lissa and picked up my wayward feline. "I think we'd better get her home before something else scares her, and she's gone for another day."

"Everyone will be so glad to see her." Lissa had a big smile on her face.

I cuddled that silly cat in my arms as we walked home, keeping a firm grip. No way was I going to let her get loose.

And odds were good that Lissa would never, ever

leave that door open again.

I looked over at my aunt as we reached our house. "Thanks for helping me find her."

"It was the least I could do. I really am very, very sorry."

"I know. It's okay." And I pretty much meant it.

Tasha was safe, and that was the important thing. We entered the kitchen, and Lissa carefully closed the door behind us.

I dumped a bunch of the tuna in Tasha's bowl and let her chow down. Then I called Kat to let her know that Tasha was safe. Kat had been sleeping but didn't mind waking up to good news. I called Mom and left a message on her cell phone, so she wouldn't have to worry anymore.

Dad? Nah, he could find out when he got home.

After making the calls, I got out a towel and dried off my bedraggled pet.

She didn't like that part much and struggled to get free. When I let her go, she trotted behind the couch.

Thank You, God. Thank You.

With Tasha safe, I could concentrate on my other dilemma.

I stuck the package of pictures and the memory card from my broken camera in my pack, then went over to peek behind the couch.

Tasha was curled into a tight black ball, her fluffy tail softly twitching. She should be okay for a bit without me.

"I'm going to the camera shop to see if Mr. Browning can make me a rush, rush order," I told Lissa. "I have to turn my entries in by five today, so that

179

doesn't give me much time."

"Oh, that's right. I'd forgotten they were due today. I can drive you to the shop."

"Thanks, but I'll take my bike. Though I could use a ride to the fair later, if Mom doesn't get home in time."

"I'd be happy to."

I bet she would. It might take a few good deeds to make her feel better about letting Tasha get out. Smiling, I checked on my cat one last time

The sky always seemed bluer and the leaves greener after a rain, and the morning sun lit up the wet grass like a field of jewels. The breeze cooled my face as I rode along. The day had started out well; maybe my luck would hold. If I could get a few of those pictures replaced—even just the ones of Gram—I would still have a chance to win the camera.

Would it be wrong to pray for a camera? It did seem kind of selfish.

I looked up at the sky with a questioning gaze, in case God was watching. But I didn't say anything out loud.

Mr. Browning was in the back section of the store helping an older man and lady when I got there, so I waited as patiently as I could. It was ten thirty, and the later it got, the less chance I had. *Please hurry up, people.*

They bought a lens and some lens cleaner and left the store.

I hurried to the counter.

"Well, JJ, how nice to see you again so soon," Mr. Browning said with his friendly smile. "What can I do for you?"

"You're not going to believe what happened …"

"Don't tell me you lost the pictures again."

"Not exactly. But my cat got lost and I had to go look for her and I left the pictures out in the rain." The words came out in a rush. I opened the package and showed the pictures to Mr. Browning.

"Oh, dear," he said. "What a shame!" He came to the ones of Brett. "Well, at least you have two you can use. And you have the first batch of pictures, right?"

I nodded. "But the ones of my great-grandma are the best. I need to replace those."

"I might be able to help. I deleted files from the computer yesterday, so I'll need your memory card."

I handed it to him.

He slipped it into the computer and clicked a couple of keys. Waited, then clicked again. "Hmm. It doesn't seem to be working. Let me clean it off." Mr. Browning blew some air on the card and tried again.

Nothing.

"What's wrong with it?" I grabbed the edge of the counter and leaned across.

An error message flashed on the screen.

He pulled it out again and studied it. "This is from the camera that got broken, right?"

I nodded.

"I'm afraid the memory card was damaged too. My computer can't read it." He handed me the card.

My heart sank to the floor. "But it has to work."

Mr. Browning patted my hand. "I'm really sorry, but it's something I can't fix."

"Can anyone fix it?" There had to be something I could do.

"I don't know. Maybe a computer expert."

And where would I find someone like that in time to get photos made today? "Thank you," I whispered, working to keep my voice steady. I took the package and walked out of the store.

One big cloud had moved in to block the sun. The buildings around me turned gray in its shadow.

A quick shiver ran through me as the chilly breeze swept past.

Without the photographs of Gram, I had no chance to win the grand prize. And without the grand prize, I had no camera. I did have a big lump of cement in my chest, though, and I didn't know how to break it open.

27

I leaned against my bike outside the photo shop, trying to decide what to do. *God, please help. You don't have to make me win the contest if You don't want to. Tell me what to do.*

The soft breeze kept blowing, the sun shining. No bright lights or voices from heaven.

But I had an idea. Maybe I should try the retirement home again. True, I'd already searched twice, and the lady said she'd call me if the pictures showed up, but I had to do something. Could that be God's answer?

I rode to Big Maples, locked my bike to the rack, and did another sweep of the parking lot. I looked under all the bushes out front too. If anybody peered out a window, he or she would probably wonder about the weird kid climbing under the bushes.

Nothing.

I walked inside to the reception desk.

"JJ, how are you doing?" the familiar lady asked. "I miss your great-grandma. She truly lit up the place."

I took a deep breath.

The lady leaned forward. "She was always so cheerful. And I never heard her say a bad word about anyone. She could come up with something nice to say even about the grumpiest old men. We all miss her." She smiled.

"Me too." I tried to swallow the lump in my throat.

I looked around the room, imagining Gram walking through, saying nice things to everyone. Could I be like that someday? It didn't sound easy. I wiped at a tear and turned back to the receptionist. "My pictures haven't turned up, have they?"

She shook her head. "No, sorry."

"Okay. Thanks." My shoulders sagged as I turned back toward the door. I'd probably never come through those doors again.

It might be nice to go through the building one more time, to see the places Gram hung out.

"Okay if I walk around a bit?" I asked.

"Of course. As much as you want. The residents always enjoy having a young person on the premises."

I strolled through the lobby with its fireplace and comfy stuffed chairs. Gram and I used to sit there and laugh about funny things I had seen or done. One little bald man sat there, reading a newspaper. I headed to the recreation room. Gram had spent a lot of time there, putting together jigsaw puzzles, playing cards with her friends, or just visiting—and maybe cheering people up and helping them forget their aches and pains.

A couple of gray-haired men were playing cards, a woman was knitting, and one dark-haired lady bent over a puzzle. She had been helping Gram with a puzzle that day I visited not so long ago.

Wasn't her name Elsie?

She looked up as I walked over. "Hello, dear. You're Rose's great-granddaughter, aren't you? What brings you here today?"

"I felt like looking around a bit."

"Well, I must say, I certainly miss Rose. She was such fun. And she was much better at these puzzles than I will ever be. I could use her help!" She chuckled.

Gram *had* been good at puzzles. She used to say they kept her mind sharp.

"She was so good to all of us," Elsie said quietly. "To Rose, we were all family, and I'm sure you know how much family meant to her."

Yes, I did.

Elsie pointed at me with one finger. "You know, I think I have something of yours."

"Something of mine?" What could Elsie have of mine?

"Well, maybe not, but I think it might be. Could you come to my room with me?"

"Sure."

Elsie took her cane and pushed herself out of the chair. I followed as she tottered down the hallway. "Sorry I'm so slow, dearie. Arthritis, you know."

"That's okay. I'm in no rush."

When we got to her room, she unlocked the door and let me in. She walked toward the living room.

Piles of magazines and mail covered one table—not as neat as Gram's apartment. But a nice, spicy smell made Elsie's place feel homey.

"I kept meaning to turn this in, but my memory isn't what it used to be. I found it on the floor the day Rose died."

A wild hope sprang up inside me. Could it really be? Was it possible?

When Elsie turned around, her hands held a big, fat manila envelope.

"My photographs!" I cried. "You found my photographs!" Tears of joy stung my eyes.

"I'm so sorry I didn't get them to you earlier. I figured they had to be yours with the pictures of you and Rose. But I kept forgetting." She handed me the package.

I pulled out the pile of photographs. They were still in perfect condition, all ready to turn in for the contest. I gave Elsie a big hug, almost knocking her over. "Thank you so much. I'm entering these in the county fair, and today is the final day to enter. I thought they were lost forever." I danced around the room, laughing.

Elsie leaned on her cane, looking a little puzzled but happy. "Sweetie, will you come back and tell me if you win? I'd love to see you again."

I hadn't expected to return to the retirement home, now that Gram was gone. And yet, talking with Elsie made me feel like Gram was nearby, watching and smiling. "Sure, I could do that." I hugged the envelope to my chest as I walked back to my bike.

Thank you, God! Thank You. You gave me back my cat and my photographs. You do believe in me after all. On the way home I stopped at Ray's Camera Shop to tell Mr. Browning what had happened.

He grinned from ear to ear. "I'm so happy for you, child. You go enter those pictures, and I wish you all the best."

I pedaled home as fast as I could and ran into the house, stopping to shut the door securely behind me, then raced down the hall. "I found them, Lissa! I found my pictures!" I screamed before I even reached our room.

186

Picture Imperfect

Brett's door opened.

I slid to a stop in front of him. "Brett, I found the pictures."

"Glad to hear it. When I heard the screaming, I thought Tasha got loose again or something."

"No, it's good screaming this time."

Lissa's head appeared in the bedroom doorway. "What's this I hear?"

I held up the envelope, grinning.

Lissa cheered and clapped her hands. "Oh, JJ, I'm so happy for you." She hugged me. "And I have more good news for you. I've been looking online for apartments, and Thomas will help me check them out this weekend. He said he'd lend me the money if I didn't have enough for first and last month's rent. So I will be out of your room very soon."

I smiled as we walked into the bedroom. "It actually hasn't been *that* bad sharing a room with you. Except for the Tasha thing. But I don't think that will happen again."

Lissa shook her head back and forth, eyes wide. "Oh no. I guarantee I will never forget to close the door again."

I laughed. I had my pictures and my cat, and life was good. I could forgive and maybe forget. I ran to call Kat and tell her the good news. Then I sorted through the photos one more time, selecting the best ones for the contest. It was hard looking at the pictures of Gram. How could she be gone when she looked so alive in the photographs? I took the picture of her looking out the window and set it on my dresser. That one was just for me.

That afternoon Lissa drove me to the fairgrounds to enter my photographs. As I stood in line to register, I tried to see what kind of pictures other people were entering. To win the grand prize, I would have to beat not only the other kids, but the adults, as well. And some of the grownups had probably been shooting pictures since they were my age.

The young guy in front of me had a seascape that looked real enough to splash anyone who got too close. The older lady behind me had some wonderful photos of birds, the kind of pictures only a good telephoto lens could capture. One teenage boy had photos of a soccer game that took me right into the action. The facial expressions were great. Someday, maybe I could take pictures like that too.

"They all look so good," I whispered to Lissa. "There's no way I'm going to win."

"Hey, don't be discouraged." Lissa gave me a quick one-armed hug. "Yours are really good too."

"Maybe." Or maybe not.

I wished I could talk with everyone around me and find out how they did it, what secrets they had learned over the years, what I could do to improve—once I actually had a camera again. But, judging by the quality of the pictures I saw around me, I wouldn't be the one going home with a new camera on Saturday night.

28

After we got back from submitting my photos, I opened Gram's Bible to another of the bookmarks. This one was at Luke 15. It told about a lost sheep and how the shepherd looked everywhere and got so excited when he found it that he called all his neighbors to tell them.

Prickles ran up and down my back. Had Gram known I would read that section today?

That was silly, though. She didn't even know I would take her Bible, and she certainly couldn't know what would happen today. But it reminded me about how excited I had been when we found Tasha, and how I had called Kat and Mom, so they could be excited too. And it sure seemed like I was supposed to read those verses today.

The next section was about someone losing a coin and finding it again. That woman also called her friends and neighbors to rejoice with her. Kind of like me dancing around in Elsie's apartment when she gave me my lost photographs. That must be how the lady in the Bible felt.

That wasn't the end of the Bible story. It said that rejoicing like that happens in heaven when a sinner repents. Gram had told me that repenting meant turning around—like turning away from bad things and back toward God. I could almost see Gram in heaven looking down and waiting for people to turn back to God. And she would definitely be cheering and singing with the angels whenever it happened. That would be just like Gram.

When Mom and Dad got home, they were happy to know that Tasha was alive and well, and that I had found the photos—or, rather, that Elsie had found them and returned them to me. I guess you could say they rejoiced with me right there in the kitchen.

After giving me a big hug, Mom stepped back and held up a plastic grocery bag. "I stopped at the bank and got what was in Gram's safety deposit box."

What could it be? The bag didn't seem to have much in it.

Dad, Brett, and Lissa gathered around.

Mom pulled out a small book with a faded black cover. "It's an old diary of Gram's. From the date, it looks like she was twenty-three when she started it."

"Deep, dark secrets?" Brett asked. "I mean, why would she keep it in a safety deposit box and not in a drawer in her desk?"

Mom put the book down, opened the cupboard, and grabbed a stack of plates. "After dinner, we can take a look. I haven't had time to open it yet."

"I wonder what Gram was like when she was twenty-three," I said. "It's hard to imagine her that young."

"Was there anything else in the box?" Lissa asked.

"A few photographs. That's it."

"Photographs? What kind of photographs?" That word always caught my attention.

"Let me see." Dad reached into the bag.

Mom looked over his shoulder. "They're family pictures. Gram and Gramps and a baby—probably my mom. A few from when Mom was older, and a couple when Lissa and I were babies. And one of our family of four when JJ was missing a tooth."

Dad took a quick glance and started to put them back.

I reached up. "May I see them?"

He handed the pictures to me, and Lissa came over to look too.

Mom was right; they were pretty ordinary family pictures. I flipped the one of us over to see if it had a date on the back. "Mom? Why does it say 'treasure'?"

Mom took the picture and looked at the back. "I have no idea."

Gram was full of mysteries.

I wanted to find out what was in the diary, but Mom made us eat dinner—a quick meal of tuna rice casserole and cooked carrots—first. After eating, we cleared the dishes and gathered back at the kitchen table as if drawn by the curious diary.

Mom flipped through the pages first to get an idea of what might be in there. As she did so, something fell out. Mom picked it up and showed it to us.

It was another photograph, yellowed with age, this one of a young man in a suit who held a baby girl in a frilly white dress.

"That must be Gramps holding our mother," Lissa said.

Mom shook her head. "No, Lissa. Look more closely. Gramps had dark hair. This man's hair is blond."

"Hmm, and it doesn't really look like the other

191

picture of Gramps—or any picture of Gramps that I've ever seen."

Mom turned it over. "It says 'William with Jane at age one.'"

I sat up straighter. "Who are William and Jane? I didn't know we had a Jane in the family." Was that where my middle name came from?

"I don't know who they are." Mom looked baffled. "But Gram was the one who suggested your middle name, so maybe your name did come from this Jane." She stared at the picture. "I think we had better do some reading."

Brett's eyes brightened. "This is cool. I can't wait to hear what Gram had to say."

Dad scooted his chair back from the table and crossed his ankles, settling in.

Mom opened the book to the first page. "There's an extra page glued in here. Let me read it." She held it close and squinted.

Gram's handwriting had gotten a bit scratchy in the past couple of years, and this pasted-in page looked recent.

"'Perhaps I should have told you all about this part of my life before,'" Mom read. "'My dear husband, James, knew about it. But once we moved from Minnesota out here to Oregon, none of our friends knew. I just kept it in my heart. It wasn't so much a secret as something I no longer needed to talk about. But now I want to share this diary. First, so you will understand better where my faith came from, and second, so you will know these dear ones of mine when you meet them in heaven—as I will likely do soon.'"

The last line made my eyes feel suddenly hot. I blinked a couple of times, thinking about Gram in heaven.

"Wow. What kind of a secret could Gram have?" Brett asked. "Weird."

Who were these people we would meet in heaven? "Start reading," I begged. "Please."

"'January twenty-third. I lost my family today, and it's all my fault.'"

We stared at her. What on earth?

Mom's face got pale, but she kept on reading. "'I wanted some time to myself. Little Jane had been teething and was so very fussy. My sweet husband offered to take her for a ride in the car to give me a break. When I heard the sirens in the distance, I knew it was William and Jane. And then, when I saw the police car outside, I barely had the strength to open the door. The officer said the car hit some black ice and ran into a tree. They were both killed instantly. Now I am alone with my guilt, and it's more than I can bear.'"

29

Mom stopped reading and sat still as one tear rolled down her cheek.

For a long moment, no one said a word.

Dad spoke up. "You mean your grandma was married before—and had a baby you never knew about?"

Mom nodded. "It appears so."

"So," I said quietly, "I was named after Gram's baby." Who would have thought Gram could have a secret like that? I felt kind of spooked inside, like I had just seen a ghost.

"Read more," Lissa said. "Or I'll read if it's too hard for you."

"I'm fine. It just took me by surprise." Mom wiped her eyes. "'January twenty-fourth. The pastor stopped by today. He told me that God can use all things for good, even something as tragic as this. I don't know if I believe him. I feel like I'm being sucked into the darkness with no way out. But I agreed to be open for one year to what God does in my life. If God can bring any good out of this horrible tragedy, then I will serve Him forever.'"

"He must have," I said, thinking about the Gram I knew. "Gram did serve God all her life, so He must have made some good things happen."

"You may be right," Mom said.

That evening no one cared about watching TV or playing video games or listening to music. We all sat together at the kitchen table, taking turns reading—because Mom started losing her voice after a while—and listening to Gram's story. In one place in the journal, she called it a story of her "inner journey to God."

And God did bring good out of it, although Gram had some really bad days too. At the funeral, one man realized that he didn't know how much time he had left and rededicated his life to God. Gram got to know the people of the church as they brought food and spent time with her. Gram became closer to her parents and brothers and sisters as they helped her in her pain. Later, when the baby of a young mother in Gram's neighborhood got sick and died, Gram was able to help because she understood what that mother was going through.

And all through the diary were times when she talked about growing to love God more and about how the deep pain of the tragedy opened her to the joy of little things. How she never really appreciated the delicate patterns on a butterfly's wings before, or the different shades of green in the spring. In fact, noticing that beauty made her take up painting, and she seemed to find a lot of comfort in her art.

Lissa was reading when we came to the last page, January 23 of the next year. "'I met a young man recently. His name is James. He is a quiet, gentle man, whose fiancée fell off a horse and died three years ago. We understand each other in a way other people cannot. I think God brought us together. As I look back on the past year, I realize that the pastor was right. God did bring good things out of the tragedy. And so, I will keep my promise. I will serve God for the rest of my life—with all my heart.'"

"Wow." I had always loved Gram, but now I admired her even more. So many emotions swam through me that I wasn't even sure what to say. I sat there, lost in thought about Gram and God and life. How could the world be so full of beauty and pain and many other things I had never really noticed before? What other mysteries were still out there to learn?

"And that James was Great-Grandpa," Brett said. "We never would have existed if Gram hadn't lost her first family and met him."

"Yes." Lissa closed the journal. "That had to be the same James, because she got married the next year."

Mom stood up and looked at the clock. "I need to get busy. Lots happening tomorrow. My mom and dad arrive in the afternoon, and Alan, Sara, and the kids in the evening. And I'll have to get things together for the memorial service on Sunday."

"Thomas will be arriving too." Lissa's eyes sparkled.

"I have a baseball game," Brett said.

"And I'm going to the fair. You can still take me, right, Mom?"

"I'll drop you and Kat off at the fair in the morning." Mom yawned and stretched. "I'll buy you both all-day ride tickets and even give you money for lunch."

I pumped a fist in the air. "Yes!"

"And I'll try to get back there before they announce the winners. That's at three o'clock, right?"

I nodded. That would be the scariest moment of the

day. Far scarier than any of the rides.

Mom dropped Kat and me off at the fair at 10:30 the next morning. The sky was clear and the temperature cool enough that we knew it shouldn't get over eighty. Perfect for a day at the fair. The smells of greasy burgers and buttered popcorn filled the air, along with high-pitched shrieks from the direction of the roller coaster and the general sound of kids having fun.

Kat wanted to head straight for the rides, but I had other plans.

"First, we have to check out my competition," I said. So we headed over to the photography display, housed in a little wooden building off to the side of the carnival area.

Photos covered the walls. More than I had expected for a county fair.

I gulped and looked around for the kids' section. I wanted to see how my pictures looked on the wall. I found the right area.

What a variety! Everything from the Grand Canyon—somebody must have gone on vacation—to little mushrooms growing in the forest were entered under Landscape. Really? Mushrooms? My waterfall looked pretty good next to the other pics. In the building category it didn't look like I had much chance. Somebody had entered some neat shots of skyscrapers glittering in the sun and others of an old courthouse, framed by oak trees. Sports included everything from bowling to hang gliding.

But I still liked the expressions of Brett and his friend. I had a chance there. I wandered past the horses and dogs and pigs and smiled at my picture of Tasha. And finally, there were the people pictures. I had entered one of Kat on the swings, one of Gram and me, and that one of Gram's hands and mine.

Mr. Browning had said those were my best shots at winning.

I stared at the one of Gram's hands, imagining those hands young and holding baby Jane. I took a deep breath. Thoughts of Gram still made me blink back tears.

"Your pictures look good. Especially the one of me." Kat gave me a big wink. "Remember, I get a cut if that one wins any money." She looked toward the door. "So can we hit the rides?"

"Not yet. I'll have to beat the adults too, to win the camera. Let's take a quick look at those."

Kat followed me without much enthusiasm. Photography wasn't really her thing, but she was a true friend.

I grinned at her to let her know I appreciated her sacrifice.

Some of the photographs in the adult section were really, really good. My insides were doing jumping jacks. I saw an especially beautiful shot of the ocean at sunset and a touching one of a mare licking her newborn colt. But my joy plummeted when I remembered these were my competition. What had made me think a newbie like myself, with a crummy camera, could win against experienced adults with cameras that cost a thousand dollars or more?

And yet the photographs were *so* beautiful. They gave me ideas for new pictures and ways of capturing emotions on film.

But that couldn't happen until I got a camera. I sighed.

Kat looked over. "Time for the rides? They would cheer you up."

"Time for the rides."

Kat screamed in excitement, causing half a dozen people within earshot to jump.

I hurried her out the door before we could get in trouble.

When it came to rides, I liked to start easy and work my way up, saving the big roller coaster that does a loop-de-loop for last. However, Kat liked to jump right in on the scariest ride so that everything else felt tame in comparison. We compromised by saving the roller coaster for later, but starting with the Screaming Eagle, where we sat, legs dangling, on a huge pendulum that swung back and forth, higher and higher until we were pretty much upside down. We screamed until we were hoarse, then ran back in line to ride it again.

After that we relaxed a bit on the Ferris wheel, enjoying views of the river nearby and the fairground around us. Kat always shut her eyes as we came over the top, but I looked out over the treetops. Looking down was what made it freaky.

I told Kat all about Gram's diary, and she lit up when I mentioned the word "treasure" on the back of our family photo.

"Treasure? *Treasure?* Maybe Gram hid some buried treasure somewhere." She slapped me on the leg as we rotated down from our high perch.

"Where could she bury treasure? She lived in an apartment."

"Maybe she hid it in her apartment, then." Her voice got low and excited. "Maybe she saved up thousands of dollars and hid the stash for your family to find. You would have enough to buy that camera."

"I don't think Gram had thousands of dollars."

We came to a stop and hopped out of our seats.

We took a turn on the little kids' roller coaster, then the Octopus that swings up and down and all around. After that we felt a bit dizzy, and it was time for lunch, so we took a break. We bought hot dogs, fries, and milk shakes and sat down at a little table to eat. We were just finishing when I heard someone call my name.

Lissa headed our way, dressed in shorts, a pink blouse, and, of course, those high-heeled shoes of hers.

What was more interesting was the guy holding her hand. He was tall, with blond hair down almost to his shoulders. His polo shirt revealed strong arm muscles. As they got closer, the brightest blue eyes I had ever seen looked my way. Lissa definitely had good taste in men.

"JJ!" she cried. "We went by to look at your photos. They look wonderful."

"You are obviously a young lady of great talent," he added.

My cheeks grew warm, and I smiled at him.

"Oh, Thomas, this is JJ and her friend, Kat," Lissa said. "And, JJ, I'm sure you already figured out who this is."

"Nice to meet you." Thomas shook my hand, then

Kat's.

Kat winked at me.

"And thanks for sharing your room with Lissa. She says you've been a wonderful roommate."

I blushed. "Well, not all the time."

"Nobody's perfect." Thomas gave me a big smile.

Okay, I never had cared much about boys before, but this Thomas was definitely hot, as Kat would say. And nice too.

"We're going to check out the fair a bit," Lissa said. "We'll be back at the photo exhibit before the awards are announced." She smiled and looked over at Thomas. A lovey-dovey look if I ever saw one.

And he looked at her the same way. Maybe he *would* move to Oregon.

"Good luck," Lissa added, looking back at me.

Kat and I waved good-bye to Lissa and Thomas, who drifted out of sight on their own little cloud.

"Nice." Kat stared after Thomas.

I nodded. Yeah, definitely nice. We headed back to the rides, starting out on the easier ones this time so our lunch could settle. Around two o'clock we made it to the big roller coaster, and it was just as fun and just as terrifying as I remembered. Kat and I got in our full quota of screams, as did most of the other people in our car. Then, of course, we did it again. But even in all the fun, my stomach tightened with dread.

Soon it would be time for judging. And tomorrow, the memorial service for Gram. And I couldn't stop either from coming.

At about a quarter till three, we wandered back to the photography exhibit. A crowd was beginning to gather, probably most of them entrants or their family members. Were the judges somewhere in the crowd, still making up their minds? I looked around. What would a judge look like? Or perhaps they had already decided and were getting the ribbons ready. My stomach churned and did flips and flops.

30

As Kat and I moved through the photography exhibit area, I saw Mr. Browning talking to a boy and girl. I made my way toward him through the crowd and Kat followed.

Mr. Browning waved me over. "JJ, good to see you. I'd like you to meet a couple of my students, Ben and Maria." He motioned toward the two kids standing at his side.

Ben was tall and skinny, with brown hair and a nice smile. Maria was shorter, with shiny, black hair and excited-looking eyes.

"Hi, JJ," they said in unison.

I smiled back at them. They looked like people I would like to spend time with, especially if it were time studying photography. If only I could take his class too. Why did everything cost money? Sometimes life seemed really unfair. I swallowed back the wave of disappointment that washed over me. "This is my friend, Kat."

Kat grinned and waved at everyone.

Mr. Browning glanced toward the door. "It looks like the judges are coming. They'll put up the ribbons in the eighteen-and-under divisions first, so you'd better go watch."

I thanked him and pulled Kat along as I followed the judges—a gray-haired woman, a bald man, and a young man with red hair.

They started with Buildings.

Sweat beaded on my forehead.

A picture of an old barn, mossy-roofed and surrounded by autumn leaves, took first place. One of the skyscrapers took second.

As I expected, I didn't win anything there. Still, a quick flash of disappointment shot through me.

Next came Sports. Ben won first prize with a picture of runners crossing the finish line. The judges walked right past my photos of Brett. Nothing there either.

What if I didn't win anything at all? Maybe I wasn't really any good at photography.

Kat squeezed my hand. "You'll win in the next section. I know you will."

I tried to smile, but it didn't quite work. Where was Mom? She said she'd try to get here. I was turning into a six-year-old on the first day of school, and I wanted my mommy.

And where were Lissa and Thomas?

I shook my head. Probably lost in their own world somewhere.

Next came the animal category. Maria took first place, with a photo of a dog and cat sleeping together. When the judges walked past my picture of Tasha to pin the second place ribbon next to a shot of a baby goat, everything started getting hazy.

But they turned back. The gray-haired lady holding the white ribbon stopped in front of Tasha.

My breath caught in my throat. *Yes, please, please.*

She pinned it to the wall right next to my picture!

My heart starting beating again, and I gasped. A

ribbon. I had won a ribbon!

"Yes!" Kat pounded me on the back. "You got one!"

"It's just third place." But hope had returned. If I could win one ribbon, I could win more. I grinned at Kat and followed the judges on to Landscapes. As we neared the area, I felt a hand on my back and turned to see Lissa, Thomas in her wake.

"You got a ribbon!" Lissa cried. "I got here just in time to see it. Have you won any others?"

Her eyes were shiny, and it turned me warm inside.

Thomas gave a thumbs-up.

"No others yet. But they're not done."

My waterfall got an Honorable Mention.

Not bad, but I had hoped for more.

"Probably should have stuck that one of me in," Lissa said with a lopsided grin.

Maybe I should have. That hot dog wasn't digesting too well. One category to go, and the best I had was a third-place prize.

Finally, we arrived at People. I looked at Kat, and she looked at me. We both crossed all the fingers we could.

Lissa put her hand on my shoulder.

It was my last chance. I needed a first-place ribbon to be eligible for the grand prize. *Please, God.*

The judges took a quick look around again.

I held my breath, and my heart did a tap dance in my chest.

This time, the judges started with third place. Maria took third with a picture of a baby splashing water at the edge of a lake. Somebody I didn't know won second with a back view of an older couple holding hands as they walked down a path in some park. The bald man held the blue ribbon and glanced up and down the line of pictures.

I froze where I was.

He walked over to my photograph of *Hands* and stared at it for what seemed like hours. Then he reached up and pinned the blue ribbon to the wall right next to it. "First place goes to Jada Jane Monroe," he announced.

Kat jumped up and down. "Yes, yes! You won!" she screamed.

The judge and part of the crowd turned to look.

I shook my head at her, finger to lips, but I was grinning the whole time.

Kat settled down and gave me a high-five.

Lissa and Thomas both hugged me.

Mr. Browning gave a thumbs-up from across the crowd.

A warm glow filled me. I had won first place! The squeals of excitement that drifted in from the carnival rides echoed my exhilaration. I had won. Better than that, Gram and I had won together. I glanced up at the ceiling, half expecting to see Gram smiling down at me from heaven.

"Now we will move on to the adult categories," the bald man announced.

"Does that mean you don't get Grand Prize?" Kat asked, suddenly solemn.

"They probably give that out at the very end, after all the adult categories." I took a deep breath. I looked over at Lissa, who nodded.

"Yes, I think that's how they do it."

We followed the judges as they moved on.

"JJ!" Mom made her way through the crowd. "Did I make it in time? Have they announced the winners yet?"

"JJ won first prize in People," Kat crowed. "But not with the one of me." She put on an exaggerated frown.

"I won a first, a third, and an honorable mention," I told Mom. That was good, wasn't it? Better than nothing at all, that's for sure.

"She did really great for her first contest." Lissa smiled at me.

"Oh, JJ, how exciting. I'm so proud of you." Mom gave me a big hug, which warmed me all over.

"They haven't announced the grand-prize winner yet. They're doing the adult categories first."

"Well, let's stick close by, then," Mom said, "so we don't miss the announcement."

I crossed my fingers and listened as the category winners were announced. They were all really great photographs. Would mine be good enough? I needed that camera!

The young judge spoke this time. "We will now award the grand-prize winner. This was a very difficult decision, as there were so many wonderful photographs entered. I wish we had more than one to award." He motioned toward the lady judge, who was holding a big purple ribbon with a golden rosette at the top.

Hot and cold waves washed over me, hope and fear churning me around like I was lost in a washing machine. Time stood still, and all my life seemed focused in a bright circle around that judge, a picture of uncertainty. Would this moment's picture be titled *Dreams Fulfilled* or *Hope Lost*? I held my breath and

207

waited.

"Remember," the lady judge said, "winners should pick up their prize money at the front desk before leaving today. Congratulations to all the winners. And, to those who didn't make it this year, please come back and try again next year." She held up the grand-prize ribbon.

My heart jumped, and my head pounded.

"And now … I am pleased to award the grand prize to Mr. John Robley for his fine photograph, *Mount Hood Dawn*."

The crowd clapped as Mr. Robley stepped forward to shake hands with the judges.

I felt myself falling, falling down from the clouds into darkness.

His picture *was* amazing—the colors of the sunrise in the sky with Mt. Hood in the background and a doe and her fawn stepping out into some misty mountain meadow. It was better than anything I had done or even knew how to do. But that didn't stop me from wanting to crash through the floor. That wonderful camera would not be mine.

Mom put an arm over my shoulders. "I'm sorry you didn't win," she said softly.

Lissa reached out to touch my arm, her face sad.

"Yours was way better," Kat declared.

"No, it wasn't." It wasn't, and it never would be. How could I get better without a camera, without someone to teach me? It was hopeless. I pushed Mom's arm away, as the world around me turned blurry and out-of-focus. I bit down on my quivering lower lip. My eyes were hot, and the crowds were crushing me. I had to escape. I stumbled toward the door, my walk becoming a trot, bumping into people and not bothering to apologize. When I reached the door, I sprinted away, not even caring which direction I ran. I had to get away.

31

I almost ran over a little boy licking an ice cream cone, but caught myself in time.

The woman holding his hand glared at me.

I mumbled a quick, "Sorry," and stumbled on, but slower now. As I left behind the flashing lights and happy screams, the people thinned out, and I could breathe again. I walked past the picnic area toward the bluff overlooking the river, my heart still pounding. Breathing hard, I flopped down onto my back in the grass and wiped a hand across my sweaty forehead.

Why had I even hoped I could win? Me, a beginner who didn't really know what she was doing? How stupid.

Towering, white cumulus clouds glided across the blue sky above me. As the formations drifted, I made a picture frame with my hands and moved it around, setting up the photos I couldn't take. My throat ached. *Gram, can you see me from heaven? Do you know how much I miss you? What about You, God? Gram said You believe in me. It doesn't feel like it now.* I sat up and swallowed hard, but the ache didn't go away.

"JJ!" The voice sounded far away.

I ignored it. I wasn't going back to hear Kat say how I should have won and Mom tell me I might get a new camera for Christmas. None of that would really help one bit.

"There you are, JJ." A man's voice.

Lissa and Thomas walked toward me. Great. Just what I needed. I turned away toward the river.

Lissa's sweet perfume filled the air as she plopped down beside me and put an arm around me.

Half of me wanted to push it away, but the other half wouldn't let me.

Thomas walked back toward the fair, leaving us alone.

"Thomas is going to let your mom know we found you," Lissa said quietly. "She was pretty worried when you ran off."

"I didn't win." I stared down at the grass. "I don't know why I thought I could. What do I know about photography?"

Lissa rubbed my back. "You have a lot of talent, JJ. You won first place with the picture of you and Gram, remember? She would be so happy for you. And so proud."

A knife cut through my heart. "Yes, but I didn't win the camera. And I can't even tell Gram that her picture won." My eyes stung. I wasn't a little kid. I should be able to deal with my emotions. But I *felt* like a little kid right then.

"It's hard." Lissa squeezed my shoulder. "Life isn't fair sometimes. I know how you feel."

I stiffened. "How could you know?"

She spoke, very softly, and I could feel the pain in her voice. "It wasn't fair when I got fired. I really liked my job and the people I worked with—well, most of them, anyway. I didn't want to leave California, but I knew I wouldn't be able to get a job down there."

I guess she *did* know about "unfair."

She gave me a wobbly smile, her watery eyes mirroring mine.

I leaned against her.

"At least I had a place to go. I knew my big sister would take me in. Sorry about invading *your* space, though."

"It's okay," I whispered. And I meant it all the way this time. After all, if a person couldn't go to her family for help, where could she go?

"Ready to head back?"

I nodded. The sun shone on my face like Gram's smile, and her smile always made me feel better. If I could somehow keep Gram's smile inside me, everything would be all right.

Mom, Kat, and Thomas met us at the edge of the fairground. Mom came rushing over and grabbed me in a big hug, like she was trying to squeeze all the hurt out of me. Like I was a little kid again.

I didn't mind.

"Are you okay, JJ?" She drew back and looked me in the face.

"I will be." I took a deep breath. "But I wanted that camera *so* bad." My voice cracked a bit.

"I've been so focused on my school that I didn't understand how much this meant to you or how much talent you have. Your pictures are very good." She gave me an extra squeeze. "We'll save up and get you another camera. It just might take a while."

I studied Mom's face. "You really think my pictures are good? You're not only saying that because you're my mom, are you?"

Mom smiled. "I think they're wonderful."

"So do I," Lissa said.

Thomas nodded, smiling with those bright blue eyes.

"Me too." Kat punched me in the shoulder.

A cool, sweet feeling filled me up like an ice cream snack on hot day. "Gram thinks I have a God-given gift."

Mom nodded. "Gram was a wise woman. Now, why don't we go pick up your prize money and head home? Your grandma and grandpa have arrived, and the others will be coming in an hour or two."

We picked up my thirteen dollars of prize money. I gave three dollars to Kat for helping me and being a good friend, even if the picture of her didn't win, and stuck the ten-dollar bill in my pocket.

Ten dollars—not nearly enough for a camera, but it was a start. If I saved every penny I got, how long would it take to save up enough? Babysitting? Yard work? There had to be ways to earn the money. I'd figure it out later, when my head stopped hurting.

As we walked to Mom's car, the fog that had taken over my world slowly lifted. Losing the grand prize didn't hurt quite as much now. Mom thought I had talent, and she wanted to get me another camera, even though we couldn't afford it until later. My pictures had done well for my first try, and I had a family that cared about me. If my gift really was God-given, then wouldn't God provide a way for me to use it? That's what Gram would say. Still, it was going to be awfully hard waiting.

32

When Mom and Kat and I got home from the fair, Brett came trotting down the steps to greet us. We climbed out of the car as Lissa and Thomas pulled in behind us.

"How'd it go?" Brett called out. "Where are all your ribbons?"

"I did get a couple of ribbons. I can pick them up tomorrow," I said. "No grand prize, though."

"Well, you *are* just a kid. Can't expect the grand prize your first try. Kind of like expecting to make Varsity as a seventh grader."

Ouch. I knew my pictures weren't *that* amazing, but still ... He didn't have to remind me.

"Hey!" Kat screeched. "You'd better watch it, Brett."

Mom shook her head at Brett. "That's enough. JJ's photographs are wonderful."

"They really are." Lissa winked at me. "She may very well end up a professional photographer someday."

"Really?" I looked up at her. She wasn't joking, was she? "You think I could?"

"*I* think you could," Thomas said, smiling. "And I'm not even related to you. In fact, I'd love to have one of your pictures. I hear you have a special one of Lissa that might interest me." He winked.

Lissa let go of me and aimed an elbow at Thomas, but he jumped out of the way. She shook her head.

214

I laughed.

Brett raised his hands in surrender. "Okay, I'm sorry. I didn't mean anything. Anyway, Grandma and Grandpa are here. We've been waiting for you guys, so we could order pizza."

So that was why Brett had come out to meet us. Always thinking with his stomach.

"Speaking of food, it's about my dinnertime," Kat chimed in. "Gotta go. Thanks for taking me to the fair." She waved good-bye and headed home as we went inside.

My grandparents were sitting in the family room with Dad.

I ran over and hugged them both. I hadn't seen them since last summer when we drove down to California to visit.

Grandma's hair looked a little grayer, but her eyes still looked like Mom's. Grandpa's head looked a little shinier and his tummy a bit rounder, but his smile was just as big as ever.

Mom came over and hugged them too.

Dad stood up and looked at me with raised eyebrows. "So, how did it go? Did you win?"

"A couple in the kids' categories. No grand prize. So no camera."

"Well, that's a great start. I'm proud of you." He came over and hugged me.

Wow. How long had it been since Dad had hugged me? Months? A year? I smiled deep down inside and gave him a big squeeze back.

"Hang in there. Your chance will come." He patted me twice on the back and returned to his chair, looking a bit awkward.

"Your dad was telling us what a good photographer you are," Grandma said.

Another surprise. Dad bragging about me? I tried to look humble. Actually, since I hadn't won the grand prize, looking humble wasn't that difficult.

Lissa and I brought out the chairs from our room, so everyone would have a place to sit. We weren't exactly used to company. Well, except for one particular aunt.

We were still figuring out what kind of pizza to order when another car pulled into the driveway. Mom and Lissa and I scrambled up from our chairs and out the door to greet Mom's brother, Alan, his wife, Sara, and my cousins, Lara and Luci. Lara was about Brett's age, with long, dark hair and thin legs that she showed off with short shorts. Luci was a year older than me, with curly, dark hair. She was wearing makeup for the first time since I'd known her.

We showed everyone in and brought the kitchen chairs into the family room. It was definitely crowded with twelve people squeezing in. Brett made room for Lara next to him, probably glad he'd taken a shower after his game even if she was his cousin.

Luci sat by me. We used to play badminton and climb trees together, but now all she wanted to do was talk about her new boyfriend. Trying to sound grown-up, I guess. I tried to listen politely, but it wasn't easy.

Grandpa finally got the pizzas ordered. We spent most of the evening sitting around and talking. Mom shared Gram's journal with the rest of the family. Uncle Alan and Aunt Sara talked about the cruise they had gone on for their anniversary.

Was it hard for Mom and Dad to listen to their stories when the best they could do was a couple of days at the beach? If they were jealous, they didn't act like it.

Luci kept talking about that boyfriend of hers. Apparently, he got straight A's, was captain of his baseball team, and could leap tall buildings without breaking a sweat. Or at least something close to that. Luci always had been good at creative writing.

Poor Thomas didn't know anyone but Lissa, yet he smiled and held Lissa's hand. *That* was a boyfriend.

I enjoyed hearing everyone's stories for a change—well, except for that mythical boyfriend. Maybe I was growing up. Maybe Gram had slipped her love of family into my heart before she left us. Somehow, I finally felt like I belonged here. If only I could tell Gram. She would be so pleased.

After a few hours, all the out-of-towners left for their hotel—except for Thomas. Lissa replaced her high heels with walking shoes, and the two of them left to "get some air." Tasha wandered out from whatever hiding place she had found, and I helped Mom clean up and get things ready for tomorrow. At least with pizza for dinner, clean-up was easy.

As she placed the last glass in the dishwasher, Mom turned to me, a questioning look on her face. "JJ, we need some photos of Gram for the memorial service tomorrow. I was wondering if we could we use copies of the ones you took recently?"

Was it possible to hurt and feel good at the same time? I was proud that Mom wanted to use my pictures.

217

However, those pictures were the last ones I had taken of Gram. Looking at them made my chest ache and my eyes burn. Nodding, I turned away and headed back to my room. Tomorrow was going to be a rough day.

33

Sunday morning began with sunshine and warm temperatures. I took a shower and washed my hair for the service. The relatives started wandering over mid-morning, and we sat around and talked. I helped Mom fix sandwiches for everyone. Lissa actually offered to heat up some soup, maybe so she could keep an eye out the window, watching for Thomas. He arrived around noon, wearing a dark suit and a blue tie that made his eyes look even brighter.

After lunch, the rest of us separated to change into our nice clothes for the service. Tasha was sleeping on my bed, so I cuddled her for a moment before I put on a white shirt and a dark purple skirt with tiny flowers all over it. Gram had once said the skirt reminded her of a mountain meadow.

Brett and Dad wore suits for the first time in I don't know how many ages. They both kind of squirmed like they were trying to get comfortable.

I was squirming inside, but not because of my skirt. If only the clock would stop and we wouldn't have to go to the service ... But it kept moving right along, and soon it was time to leave.

We took a few pictures of Gram over to the church. Mom set them up in the reception hall, putting the one I had taken recently in the middle. *My* picture of Gram right there for everyone to see. She looked wise and loving in that photo, like her true character was shining through. People could look at it and know something about Gram.

Peering into the sanctuary as people began to gather, I stared again at those stained-glass windows. With the bright sun shining through, they glowed with many colors. In my mind, I snapped a photo of the windows and the light streams reaching toward the altar.

The white bus from Big Maples Retirement Home pulled up in front of the church, and lots of gray-haired people with canes got out, slowly making their way up the front steps, including Elsie.

I ran out to greet her.

"JJ, how are you?" She clasped my hand in her papery one. "But I suppose that's a silly question on a day like this, isn't it?"

I nodded. "Kind of. It feels so weird to be here without Gram sitting next to me in the pew."

Elsie gave me a little hug.

Mom called me and I told Elsie I had to go. Next time I saw her, I'd tell her about my winning picture.

Mom and I waited in the reception hall until the service was about to start. Mom said it was tradition for the family to go in last. Everyone seemed solemn and sad, not at all like last night when we talked and laughed together.

I was all thin and stretched out inside, like the delicate layer of ice on a mud puddle on an autumn morning, so fragile that a single footstep would shatter it into a thousand pieces.

Music began playing in the sanctuary.

Mom nodded to Grandma and Grandpa, and we all

walked slowly around to the main door. Down the aisle we went, with everyone looking at us.

Kat was sitting with her mom, toward the back. She gave me a little wave as I walked past.

Toward the front, Mr. Browning sat by himself.

I had gone to a wedding once, and people stood up to watch the bride go down the aisle. They didn't stand up for us. A wedding was a beginning; today's service was an ending.

We settled into the front seats. I ended up between Mom and Lissa. I squeezed Mom's hand and then Lissa's. We were all together, all friends, as a family should be. Just as Gram would have wanted.

Gram would have liked the service too. We sang "What a Friend We Have in Jesus" and "Amazing Grace." The pastor talked about how much he admired Gram and shared a little about her life. Mom had told him about her first family, but all he said was that she "had known great tragedy, but turned to God and became a stronger person because of it."

My face got hot and my throat tight when he talked about her life at the retirement home and how much people had liked her there. When he mentioned her art, I peeked back at Mr. Browning, who nodded his head.

Most of all, the pastor talked about Gram's heart. "She was never rich in money, but she was rich in the love of God and family."

I took Mom's hand during that part and did my best to blink back the tears. A few still leaked out, but Gram would understand.

While everyone sang, I stared up at the bright stained-glass windows, trying to look through them into heaven. Shafts of colored light seemed to shine straight into my heart. A warm, peaceful feeling settled deep into me. *God, is that You?*

Jesus wanted to come into my heart, Gram used to say. My heart felt somehow different now. I imagined Gram up in heaven, holding God's hand, smiling down at us. *God, would You please tell Gram hi for me? Tell her I believe in You too, and I'm going to see her again someday. But right now, I really miss her.*

The service ended. Before we stood to walk out, I touched Mom's arm. "Mom, do you think maybe we could go to this church? I really like it here."

Mom smiled and wiped an eye. "I think maybe we could."

I felt like Gram was hugging me then. Maybe she was even cheering with the angels.

At the reception, lots of people came up to tell us how much they liked Gram and how much they would miss her. I felt all raw inside and tired, like I had run five miles. When I saw Kat motion at me from the refreshment table, I hurried over.

"These chocolate chip cookies are really good." She handed me one.

I took a bite and found I was actually able to chew and swallow. It *was* good.

"Good service. And I like your picture over there."

"Thanks." I glanced at the door. Would anyone miss me if Kat and I slipped out and took a walk? "Let's get out of here." I nudged Kat with my elbow.

"Oh yeah." Kat grinned. "We could take off. Catch a plane for Paris." Her eyebrows jumped up and down. "Or a train for New York." She sighed and shrugged.

"Or we could just walk around the block, if you're short on time."

I laughed. What would I do without Kat? "Let's go."

Kat grabbed a lemon bar, and we headed for the back door.

I was pushing the handle when a familiar voice called out, "Kat, time to go."

We froze in place.

Kat turned and frowned. "Oops. Looks like all plans are off."

Kat's mom walked up to us. She put an arm around my shoulder. "I'm so sorry about your great-grandma, JJ. She was a fine lady."

I nodded.

She gave Kat a gentle push, and they headed for the front door.

"See you tomorrow." Kat waved back at me.

I meandered back to the refreshment table.

Brett stood near the other end of the table with a plateful of food. Our California relatives were gathered across the room, quietly talking, which made sense as they didn't know any of these people. Lissa and Thomas walked over to join them, followed by Dad. People from the retirement home were beginning to wander toward the door. Probably didn't want to miss the bus.

Where was Mom? Would this be over soon? Ah, there was Mom across the room, talking to Mr. Browning. I wouldn't be visiting his shop for a while. Not until I could save enough for a camera. As if the day weren't depressing enough already.

I turned back for another cookie. I had just finished

223

it when Mom came up, put her hands on my shoulders, and looked into my eyes. Uh-oh. This was either something very good or something very bad. I took a deep breath.

She opened her mouth as if to speak but another gray-haired lady from the retirement home headed our way, her cane tapping a rhythm on the wooden floor. "We'll talk later." Mom turned and accepted more condolences.

I wandered off, looking for a quiet place but not finding one.

At the front door, Mr. Browning was putting on his hat. "Congratulations on your ribbons at the fair, JJ. Terrific job."

"Thanks."

"And sorry about your great-grandma. Rose would be very proud of you, you know." He nodded, as if lost in thought, then looked back at me. "Someday you could be a fine photographer if you keep working at it."

That was kind of hard to do without a camera. My ten dollars from the fair was a start, but I would have to put in a lot of hours of work before I'd have enough for a decent one. How many months would that take?

"Well, take care." He turned toward the door. "See you soon."

Soon? Not likely. But I hoped it wouldn't be too terribly long.

34

I waved good-bye to Elsie as the white bus from the retirement center rolled away. Maybe in a few days I would go visit—when the sadness inside let up a little. I'd probably have to help Mom clean out Gram's apartment soon. My stomach clenched at the thought. Was it time to go home yet?

The reception area cleared out as the last visitors left. Lara and Luci were talking with Brett, who seemed to be enjoying the attention. Mom and Dad piled the photographs and other things we had brought into a box to take home. Uncle Alan and Aunt Sara carried the flowers out to their car.

"We'll meet you at the house," Uncle Alan called, motioning to Lara and Luci to join him.

Grandma came over and gave me a hug while still dabbing at her eyes. "We'll see you at home." She and Grandpa headed for the door.

Lissa and Thomas walked over, holding hands.

"Are you okay, JJ?" Lissa asked. "It's been a rough day, hasn't it?"

It had definitely been a rough day. Still, it felt good to have so much family around, even if it was for such a sad reason. Family made us rich, just like Pastor Bob said.

My eyes opened wide. "That's it." I finally got it.

"That's what?" Lissa looked confused.

"Gram wrote the word 'treasure' on the back of our family picture. The treasure is our family. That's what she was trying to say."

"Makes sense," Lissa said. "She did treasure her family." She gave me a squeeze and turned to Thomas. "Ready to go?"

He nodded, and they headed out.

A lady from the church handed Mom a big plate of leftover cookies.

When she turned and looked at me, her mouth dropped open.

Uh-oh. What now?

Mom handed the plate to Dad and headed straight for me. "JJ, I'm so sorry. I was about to tell you something, and I got distracted. It's been that kind of a day." She glanced around the room and sighed.

I nodded and waited for whatever it was she had to say.

"I talked with Mr. Browning. He was quite impressed with your photographs. He said you have a lot of talent and that you put a lot of time and thought into your pictures."

Was that all? "He told me that too."

Mom smiled. "Yes, but there's more. He wants you to join his photography class—for free." She took my hand. "You'd like that, wouldn't you?"

Like it? I would love it! Excitement rose inside me, only to hit a stone wall. "But I can't. I don't have a camera." No way around that obstacle.

"He said he has an old camera you can borrow until you get your own."

"Really? You're not kidding, are you?" Photography

classes and a camera to use until I saved up for my own? Was it possible?

Mom laughed. "Honest. He said you could start next week."

"Oh, Mom! Oh, wow!" Why was I suddenly crying? I gave her a big hug and did a happy dance, my cheeks wet with tears.

Her eyebrows creased as she narrowed her eyes. "Now you're acting like Kat. Don't scare me." She smiled.

Dad walked up, car keys in hand.

I hugged him too.

"You okay, JJ?" he asked, eyes wide.

I nodded as every emotion I ever had seemed to wash through me. If I didn't do something, I would burst. "I'll meet you at the car in a minute," I said and raced off toward the sanctuary.

Oops. Gram's voice echoed in my head. *Always walk in church.*

I slowed to a sedate, respectful walk—or as close as I could manage while my heart was beating wildly and my feet wanted to dance. I slipped into the sanctuary and onto a back pew. The windows still glowed with late afternoon sunlight. This time I focused on one that showed heaven with clouds and rainbows and angels singing. My heart's glow matched the window's.

Did You have anything to do with this, God? Did Gram tell You how much I love photography? Or did You give it to me just because You love me? Thank You, God. Thank You! You do believe in me, don't You? Gram was right. I sighed and stared at the windows, happy-sad feelings still rolling over me.

The first pictures I would take with my borrowed camera would be of the windows and the light that streamed through them onto the wooden pews. Maybe I could capture a bit of the holiness I felt here. Then I would go outside and take pictures of clouds and trees, flowers and butterflies, everything beautiful and wonderful.

Mom stood in the doorway, watching me with a smile on her face.

I would take pictures of Mom and Dad and Brett and Lissa and all the rest—Gram's treasure and mine too. I soaked in the beauty of the windows one last moment before joining Mom. *Don't worry, God. I'll be back soon. Thank You for believing in me.*

The End

Acknowledgments

My writing developed slowly and with help from so many people that I could never name them all. Family and friends have all played a part.

The rough draft of this book is the result of National Novel Writing Month, 2011, which I "won" by completing 50,000 words in the month of November. Since then it has gone through many revisions. A very special thanks goes to my critique partner, Penny Wilcox, and to my critique group: Sandy Zaugg, Donna Scales, and Melody Miller. These fine ladies caught my mistakes, suggested changes, and prayed with me when times were difficult. I can never thank them enough.

A big thank you to my wonderful publisher, Ashberry Lane, and its editors, Kristen Johnson, Andrea Cox, Tami Engle, Rachel Lulich, and Amy Smith. Sherrie Ashcraft, Christina Tarabochia, and Nicole Miller: you were so kind to a new author and helped to make this book the best it could be.

Another big thank you to Oregon Christian Writers. This organization took a beginning writer and, through workshops and writing conferences, as well as wonderful moral support, grew her from neophyte into published author.

Of course, I would have gone nowhere without the support of my family. My husband, Gary Thogerson, has been such an encouragement and support. My sons, Bryan and Erik—now grown—and daughter-in-law, Elizabeth, have also given encouragement. And a special thank you to my late aunt, Rosanne Kieselhorst, who paid for me to attend OCW summer writing conferences for many, many years. I wish she were still alive to read my book, but perhaps she is rejoicing with me in heaven.

Meet the Author

Susan Thogerson Maas got her first camera around age ten and has loved photography ever since. Her favorite subjects are nature scenes and wildflowers, but she also enjoys photographing family members, who sometimes find it annoying. Her dream in grade school was to write books for children, which proves that dreams can come true. When not taking pictures or writing, Susan can be found hiking, birdwatching, working in her vegetable garden, playing on the computer, and, of course, reading.

Come visit her at www.susanmaas.com
and sign up for the Ashberry Lane Newsletter!
www.ashberrylane.com

Other Great Books for Kids from Ashberry Lane!

The Water Fight Professional
Angela Ruth Strong

I, Joey Michaels, am the **Water Fight Professional.**

Basically this means that customers pay me to soak other people. But my super-competitive best friend is sucking all the fun out of summer. All because I made a secret bet with him.

Winning the bet wouldn't be so hard if I didn't have the following three problems:

1) My dramatic mother who feels the need to schedule every moment of summer

2) A surfer dude mailman who can't keep deliveries straight

3) The annoying neighbor girl who all my friends have a crush on

If I lose … ugh, I can't even tell you what I'd have to do. I'd rather lick a slug!

ASHBERRY LANE

ASHBERRYLANE.COM

The Snowball Fight Professional

The Snowball Fight Professional

Angela Ruth Strong

I, **Joey Michaels**, am the Snowball Fight Professional.

Basically this means that customers pay me to shoot snowballs at other people. I'll use my profits to buy Grandma a gift so impressive that she'll give me a puppy for Christmas. Unless, of course, my cousin Winston has anything to do with it ...

Earning the puppy wouldn't be so hard if I didn't have the following problems:

1) Winston stealing my employee

2) Winston getting me in trouble every time I do something wrong

3) Winston blaming me for things I don't even do

If I don't get the puppy ... ugh, Winston will get him. And Christmas should be all about what I want, right?

Angela Ruth Strong

ASHBERRY LANE

ASHBERRYLANE.COM

fun 4 HIRE   Book 1